THE SMURFS 2™

Movie Novelization

Adapted by Stacia Deutsch
Story by J. David Stem & David N. Weiss & Jay Scherick & David Ronn
Screenplay by David Stem & David N. Weiss and Jay Scherick & David Ronn and Karey Kirkpatrick

SIMON AND SCHUSTER

Simon and Schuster
First published in Great Britain in 2013 by Simon & Schuster UK Ltd
1st Floor, 222 Gray's Inn Road, London WC1X 8HB
A CBS Company
Published in the USA in 2013 by Simon Spotlight, an imprint of
Simon & Schuster Children's Division, New York.

A CIP catalogue record for this book is available from the British Library
ISBN 978-1-4711-1921-7
Printed and bound in Slovakia
10 9 8 7 6 5 4 3 2 1
Visit our websites:
www.simonandschuster.co.uk
www.smurfs.com

Chapter 1

"Once upon a time . . ." Narrator Smurf opened the storybook and began to read, "in Smurf Village, happy Smurfs were going about their happy lives completely unaware that not too far away . . ." He turned to the next page and stared for a moment at the 3-D pop-up of a dark and crumbling castle. Narrator Smurf frowned, then went on. ". . . the evil wizard Gargamel was concocting a diabolical plan."

Narrator pulled a tab and a menacing paper cutout of Gargamel wearing a flowing black robe and bold red shoes rose from the page.

Creepy background music began to play as Narrator continued. "The kind of diabolical plan that is always followed by a diabolical laugh. And that plan echoed fear through the mushroom homes of the Smurfs."

The music was too loud. Narrator couldn't hear

himself reading. He lowered the book and took a long look at the nearby band of Smurfs. Everyone had a musical instrument, except Crazy Smurf, who was playing his trumpet-mouth.

He told Smooth Smurf, the director, "Guys, guys. If you drown out the narrator, no one's gonna have any idea what's going on."

"That's cool," Smooth said in a deep voice. "We'll just give you a groove, something bluesy."

The band quickly quieted down.

Narrator cleared his throat. He pretended he was Gargamel, saying, "*I* am making my own creation—an irresistible girl to infiltrate their village and betray the Smurfs."

There was a drawing of Smurfette on the next page. But this wasn't the Smurfette the Smurfs loved. This was an old version of her with long black hair. Narrator ran a paintbrush over the image. Smurfette's pale skin turned blue.

"The Smurfs found Gargamel's creation and brought her back to their village, where her wild and naughty nature wreaked havoc."

Narrator held the pictures up so everyone could see: Smurfette knocked over Painter's ladder. She stomped on Brainy's glasses. She was destroying things on purpose!

"The Smurfs wanted her gone." Narrator unfolded a scene of Papa's mushroom home, with several angry Smurfs waiting outside. "But Papa Smurf saw the good in her. With love, kindness, playful jokes, more love, delicious fruit pies, long walks, and, of course, a secret magical formula, he turned her into Smurfette, the darling of Smurf Village."

Narrator opened a pop-up door to Papa's mushroom. Inside, there was a cardboard cutout of the new, improved Smurfette. Her hair was now blond and her smile was sincere.

Narrator Smurf smiled. "It was a day we will never forget. The day our Smurfette was reborn."

With a happy sigh, Narrator Smurf looked up. The entire village had come to hear the reading of Smurfette's story.

They were gathered at the edge of a beautiful pond. As Narrator shut the book, he pointed upward to a cliff just above the water.

Smurfette stepped into view, her smile beaming. She raised her arms and performed a perfect triple flip with a twist, landing gracefully into the water.

The Smurfs applauded wildly.

"And the Smurf family had grown one bigger." That was the end of the story.

Or was it?

Smurfette climbed out of the pond. With her back turned, she shook out her wet hair. Then she turned around.

"Stupid, trusting Smurfs!" Smurfette roared. Her face was sinister. The blond from her hair faded to midnight black. "You're ours now!" She looked down into the pond's murky depths and called, "Oh, Father!"

Lightning flashed through the sky. Gargamel rose from the pond. Water violently bubbled around him. He towered above the Smurfs like a giant.

"Well done, Daughter," Gargamel chuckled.

Panicky Smurf shouted, "It's alive! It's alive!"

The Smurfs began to run.

"She tricked us!" Handy Smurf yelled.

"She's turning back!" Greedy exclaimed as Smurfette's skin grew pasty pale.

"Smurf for the hills!" Baker rushed down a narrow path.

"The world as we know it is over!" Panicky followed Baker as Gargamel prepared to pounce.

Crazy Smurf blew his trumpet-mouth in alarm.

The Smurfs were quick, but Smurfette was faster. She got in front of them and waved an ornately carved dragon wand. A blast of blue energy threw Crazy Smurf into the sky.

Gargamel praised Smurfette. "Yes, my beautiful creation! You truly are Daddy's little girl!"

The wizard rubbed his hands together with delight.

Finally the Smurfs were his . . .

"AAHHHH!" Smurfette screamed as she awoke.

She bolted up in bed, wide-eyed and sweating.

Papa Smurf was there, sitting on the edge of her mattress. He rubbed his white beard while the bad dream faded away.

"Oh Papa." Smurfette lunged forward and threw her arms around him.

Papa held her close, patting her back until she calmed down. "There, there. It's okay. Having that nightmare again?"

Smurfette nodded, choking back her tears.

Narrator Smurf continued the story where he'd left off. He was standing at the foot of Smurfette's bed. "And so, once again, on the eve of her birthday, poor Smurfette is haunted by horrible dreams of the 'Who am I?' and 'Where did I come from?' variety, which can push even the sweetest of Smurfs to the brink of insanity—"

"Okay, Narrator Smurf. That'll do." Papa Smurf pointed at the mushroom door.

With a groan, Narrator took his storybook and left the room.

Smurfette lay back on her pillows. "Papa, every year on the eve of my birthday, I have these horrible dreams about where I came from—and it makes me wonder who I really am."

Papa took her hand in his and squeezed. "And every year I tell you: It doesn't matter where you came from. What matters is who you choose to be."

Smurfette wasn't so sure.

"Don't take this old Smurf's word for it," Papa told her. "Go out there and see for yourself. This is where you belong."

Chapter 2

In Smurf Village the Smurfs were preparing a surprise birthday party for Smurfette. They were hanging decorations and setting up games while singing their favorite smurfing song, the La La song.

Clumsy interrupted the music. "Wait, because it's Smurfette's birthday, let's sing the birthday song!"

The Smurfs all agreed and started singing again. It was the same La La song.

Grouchy was helping Gutsy hang a Gargamel-shape piñata from a tree branch.

"A little lower, Grouchy," Gutsy said. "I want make sure everyone can reach!"

Baker noticed there was a problem with his cake. A big chunk was missing. "Hey! Who smurfed a bite out of Smurfette's birthday cake?"

Greedy tried to hide his face with his hands. His

cheeks were covered with frosting. "Wasn't me," Greedy said, swallowing hard.

Brainy Smurf was arranging presents on the gift table.

"Here's my present for Smurfette's surprise party," Jokey said, stepping up and holding out a box.

Brainy refused to take it. "C'mon, Jokey. Did you really think that I, the smartest Smurf in the village, would fall for your sophomoric gag? Just give me the card."

Without arguing, Jokey pulled out an envelope from under the ribbon of his present and handed it to Brainy.

BOOM!

The envelope exploded.

Brainy's face was blackened. "Outsmurfed by the old switcheroo," he said with a groan.

"Ha!" Jokey laughed.

Just then the door to Smurfette's mushroom began to slowly creak open.

"She's coming," Panicky panicked.

"Code Blue! Code Blue!" Hefty shouted a warning.

"We're Smurfs—everything is code blue," Brainy remarked with a snicker.

"Code Yellow," Hefty said instead.

"Yellow is soothing. The color of the sun." Brainy shook his head.

"Code Red!" Hefty pointed at Smurfette, who was

heading their direction.

Brainy hid the gifts behind a grove of trees. Handy threw tarps over the decorations. All the Smurfs started whistling, trying to look casual.

As Smurfette passed by, Gusty whispered, "That was close, eh, lads?"

Brainy put his hands on his hips and tapped his toe. "Did I not warn against setting up too early and having Smurfette show up and ruin everything?"

Hefty rolled his eyes. "So what else is new?"

Smurfette didn't hear anything about the surprise party. Instead she heard Brainy say something about her ruining everything. She didn't know what he meant, but it made her sad.

Smurfette pushed aside her feelings and pretended she hadn't heard. "Hey, guys. Who wants to go for a walk with me on this special day?"

"Oh, hi, Smurfette. Special? What's special about today?" Gutsy was holding a bouquet of flowers.

"Aww, are those for me?" Smurfette asked hopefully.

"Dream on, lassie!" Gutsy thrust the flowers at Hefty. "Here, for repairing the dam."

Hefty pushed the flowers back. "I don't want 'em."

Gutsy shoved them at him again. "Take 'em, you ungrateful, overstuffed toad!"

They stomped away fighting over the flowers.

Frowning, Smurfette went next to Vanity Smurf. He was staring at himself in the mirror.

"How 'bout you, Vanity? You can look at your reflection in the pond," Smurfette suggested.

Vanity set down the mirror and said, "Kinda tired of looking at myself, Smurfette." He took one more peek in the silver glass and smiled. "As if."

"So, nobody wants to go with me?" Smurfette looked around at the Smurfs. They all quickly turned away from her. All she could see were blue backs.

Suddenly, Smurfette saw a Smurf holding a clipboard, rushing into the center of Smurf Village. "Oh, hey, Party Planner Smurf," Smurfette called out. "Anything *fun* coming up that I should know about?"

Party Planner Smurf checked the clipboard's papers. "Nope. Nothing till Smurf Break. It's going to be wild! I'll put you on the guest list."

Smurfette's spirits dropped. She hung her head sadly.

Farmer Smurf reached out and touched her back, saying, "You know, occasionally it's good to have a little alone time."

The other Smurfs agreed saying, "Yeah, go on!" and

"It's fine!" and "We don't need you here!"

"Nobody wants me." Smurfette sniffled as she turned and walked into the forest.

When Smurfette was gone, Handy Smurf said, "We pulled that off pretty good, don't you think, Clueless Smurf?"

Clueless Smurf considered the question. "She seemed pretty down. Why don't we have a surprise party for her?"

Brainy bopped Clueless on the forehead. "We *are* having a surprise party for her. Get him out of here!"

Narrator Smurf followed Smurfette down the pathway to the pond. "And with that, Smurfette walked into the woods, alone, cold, and sad."

She stopped and turned to him. "I'm sorry, Narrator Smurf. Can I just be alone with my feelings?"

Narrator Smurf explained, "I'm sorry! Just trying to help the people *understand* your feelings. Apparently, nobody wants any narration. Well, I'll just be on the other side of the forest, narrating the lives of chipmunks." He walked away.

Smurfette tossed a stone into the pond. It sank straight to the bottom. "Jeesh, maybe I really don't belong here."

Chapter 3

High above a famous opera house in Paris, there was a gigantic poster of Gargamel's wicked face and the words: GARGAMEL LE GREAT! The English translation was printed at the bottom: GARGAMEL THE GREAT!

This was the most popular show in town.

Onstage, Gargamel stood next to a volunteer from the audience. The volunteer was in a trance. "You belong to Gargamel." Waving his wand, Gargamel demanded, "Say it!"

The volunteer said, "You belong to Gargamel."

Gargamel stomped his foot. "No, I! I!"

The volunteer repeated what he was told. "I. I."

"I belong to Gargamel," the wizard commanded.

"You belong to Gargamel," the volunteer said.

"Never mind. You're a dim-witted toad!" Gargamel

was frustrated.

"You're a dim-witted toad," the man repeated.

Gargamel raised his dragon wand. "No, you are!"

A zap of blue energy immediately turned the unsuspecting volunteer into a giant six-foot toad. The audience gasped.

Gargamel smirked. "This is what I do to all the critics!"

Backstage, Azrael the cat shook his head. The cat's movement caught the toad's eye. He shot out his long, sticky tongue and slurped Azrael into his mouth.

Gargamel put his ear up to the toad's full belly. "Azrael? Are you dead?"

"Meow!" The sound echoed from the frog's stomach.

"Then get out of there!" Gargamel commanded.

The toad coughed and spit Azrael across the stage. He landed in a heap of wet, slime-covered fur.

The crowd exploded into applause, jumping to their feet for an ovation.

Gargamel swooped his cape around himself and bowed. He loved being a celebrity.

Later that night there was a special report on a popular entertainment news program. A reporter sitting at a desk looked into the camera, saying, "Yet another groundbreaking feat of illusion from the most innovative conjurer the world has ever seen. Gargamania! The magical sensation that has captivated the nation from New York to Vegas is now taking on the City of Light: Paris, France! It's a runaway success."

A short video showed Gargamel cutting a dancer in half. Her top part lay still in a covered box while her legs, in a second box, ran wildly across the stage.

"Meowww!" Azrael screeched as the legs stepped on his tail.

Nancy O'Dell returned to the screen. "This master mysterio has gone from unknown to unstoppable after his surprise discovery in New York."

The show cut to another video. This one was an old clip from the day Gargamel was discovered.

A young couple, Tommy and Trisha, was making a home video about New York City. Their friend Marc was filming them when Gargamel happened by.

Tommy appeared in the center of the cell phone video. "Hey, y'all. So, Trisha and I just showed you Central Park, and now—"

Trisha leaned into the frame. "Check it out, Tommy. Times Square. This is my town, people!"

Tommy added, "And nobody does it better than—"

Behind them, Gargamel stepped into the road.

"Yo, get outta the road, freak!" a taxi driver shouted at Gargamel while leaning on his car horn.

"How dare you call me Yo." With a quick snap of his wrist, Gargamel raised his dragon wand. A blue energy beam raised the cab off the ground.

Trisha screamed. "Whoa, whoa, whoa! Did you get that, Marc? Did you?"

"No way! Push in! Push in! Push in!" Tommy told Marc.

Marc turned the cell phone camera. "I'm pushing! I'm pushing! How is he doing that?!" he asked, recording Gargamel's magic feat.

Back in the television studio, Nancy O'Dell had the video stopped and continued the report. "From New York street performer to the new toast of Europe. The only magician ever to play the famed Paris Opera House."

When Gargamel exited the theater, a crowd was waiting for autographs.

Gargamel stopped. "Thank you, ladies and gentlemen. Nothing pleases me more than pleasing me. Now get on your knees and bow!"

The crowd laughed.

"I said BOW!"

The crowd laughed some more.

With a wave of his wand, he forced the people to bow against their will. Gargamel strolled among them like royalty.

He forced another man to his knees and used him as a step stool to get inside a horse-drawn carriage. As his buggy moved away, the magic spell was broken. Everyone applauded.

Gargamel was satisfied. He leaned back in the plush seating and poured himself a drink from the bar. The neon lights flashed a rainbow of colors as a television played while muted.

"Meow," Azrael began.

Gargamel cut him off. "Would you stop tormenting me about the essence! I extracted all I could from Papa Smurf in the kingdom of New York. How much did *you* extract?"

"Meow," the cat replied.

"*I'm* squandering it?" Gargamel protested. "You're the one rolling around in caviar and catnip all day." He glanced at the wand in his hand. "Besides, they failed to bow. That's unacceptable."

Azrael rolled his eyes as Gargamel reached beneath

his cloak and raised the vial of blue essence from a strap around his neck. The bottle was only one-fourth full.

Gargamel grinned. "Look, look, look. We still have enough left to execute my delightfully diabolical plan and to preserve your precious lifestyle." He tucked away the bottle. "Soon we'll have all the essence we could ever dream of." Gargamel laughed. "So enjoyable."

Gargamel stood up and stuck his head out the sunroof. "That's right, my lowly bootlicks, you will all worship me!" he shouted to the people of Paris. Then to Azrael he said, "Including you, you flea-bitten fur bag."

Azrael gave his master a devious smile before setting his paw on the button for the sunroof.

"All hail Gargame—ACK! Stop it!" The sunroof was strangling him. "Don't break the neck that feeds you!" Gargamel gasped for air. The roof opened for a second, then closed again. "That's it! No caviar for you tonight!"

Chapter 4

Gargamel and Azrael lived in a lush five-star hotel in the heart of Paris. When they entered their huge penthouse suite, there was a box on the center of the foyer floor.

Gargamel rushed to the gift. "Ooooh, look. A present. No doubt from a worshipping admirer." The card said: 4 AZREEUHL. "Oh. It's for you."

"Meow."

Gargamel pushed the package forward. "Don't be such a scaredy-cat. It's not a trap. It's a gift. Partake!"

"Meow."

"Look, you don't want it? I'll take it." Gargamel reached out toward the box.

"Meow."

"Well, then open it, you ridiculous person." He groaned. "Cats. Can't live with them, can't serve them with cheese."

Azrael cautiously opened the box. Inside, there was nothing but a little red dot.

Suddenly the dot jumped out of the box and onto the ground. Azrael leaped on it. It moved across the floor. Azrael chased it. The dot shot over to one wall. Azrael crashed into the wall trying to get it. The dot shot to another wall. Again—*WHAM!*

Azrael wobbled away, dizzy.

WHOOSH! A pale Smurf-size creature suddenly appeared.

"Hello, kitty!"

Gargamel winked at the thing, with its bad haircut and odd appearance. "Apparently, I was wrong, Azrael. It was a trap." The tiny creature jumped onto Azrael's back.

Azrael rolled around, desperate to knock the thing off.

The thing was called Vexy. She was Smurf-size, but very pale. Vexy gracefully slid down the cat's back, grabbing on to the tip of Azrael's tail. Azrael took off, swishing and shaking.

Vexy laughed, enjoying the wild ride.

"Hackus! Hackus! Hackus!" cheered a second pale creature sitting on top of the dresser. Hackus was holding the laser pointer, adding more red dots and more chaos to the chase.

"All right. All right, children," Gargamel said, calling them to order.

Hackus jumped onto a drapery cord and swung down, knocking Azrael onto an open laundry net on the floor.

Vexy dropped the cat's tail and chuckled. "Who says cats have dignity?"

On the count of three, Hackus and Vexy tugged a rope, lifting Azrael up into the trap.

Vexy posed under the cat, hands raised in victory. "All hail Vexy—Foiler of the Felines!"

Hackus shouted, "BWAMOOOAGAGAMOOGA!"

"Well said, my idiot brother," Vexy complimented.

"Vexy! It's not nice to point out how big an idiot Hackus is. Still, it was very amusing, my little Naughties." Gargamel clapped his hands with devilish glee.

From inside the net, Azrael gave Gargamel a dirty look.

"Did we please you, Father?" Vexy asked the wizard.

Gargamel considered the question. Then replied, "No. You didn't. You know what would please me? If your putrid pale essence could endow me with real magic, like that of a true-blue Smurf. That would excite me. Instead, you're just deeply disappointing experiments."

Gargamel glanced over at Hackus, who was now hitting himself over the head with the TV remote control. He turned to Vexy. "Him more than you. Now, on to the business at hand."

Gargamel freed Azrael from the net. Azrael dropped to the ground and growled at the Naughties.

"Azrael, cease your folly and bring me my plan!" Gargamel ordered. "It's in the bathroom. On my side of the sink."

A moment later, Vexy and Hackus gathered around a tablet's blank screen. Gargamel eyed it warily. "This isn't my writing parchment," he told Azrael. "Where is my plan?!"

"Meow."

"Gone digital?" Gargamel was confused. "What does that mean?"

"Meow."

"In the Cloud?" He was even more confused. "Why would my plan be in a cloud? Are you all right? Did you concuss yourself when you hit those walls?"

Rolling his eyes, Azrael double-tapped the screen. A digital slide burst to life, complete with crude artist's renderings. The text read: "Phase 1: Create Naughties."

"Ahh, there it is. Phase One: Create Naughties." Gargamel grinned. "Check. Where's Phase Two?"

Azrael swiped the screen with a paw.

This slide said: "Phase 2: Create Portal."

There was an image of the Eiffel Tower with lightning striking it.

"Oooh. I am enamored of this swiping motion." Gargamel pushed Azrael aside and took the tablet. "Get away! And swipe . . ."

"Phase 3: Get Papa's Secret Formula."

The image was a picture of Gargamel going through a magical portal.

Gargamel rubbed his hands together. "Yes. Then Phase Three. I get the secret formula Papa used on Smurfette. . . . And swipe . . ."

"Phase 4: Turn Pale Smurfs Blue."

Gargamel ran his finger across the screen. "Then I turn you pale Naughties, and hundreds more like you, blue. . . . And swipe . . ."

"Phase 4A: Sit Back, Enjoy Plan, and Laugh."

Leaning back on the sofa, Gargamel read the text out loud. "'Sit back, enjoy plan, and laugh.'"

He swiped the screen again.

"Phase 5: Extract Essence."

A contraption appeared on the screen. All the Naughties/Smurfs were strapped into a massive, horrifying device.

Gargamel reviewed the plan. "I place you into a terrifying machine to extract your essence."

Vexy asked, "Will it hurt?"

Gargamel snorted. "No, of course not. Don't be silly." He paused. "Maybe a little. Moving on."

Gargamel quickly flipped through the remaining screens.

"Phase Six: Abuse Power." He read the small print out loud. "Details, details. 'Outlaw the cheeseburger.' 'A pox on Valentine's Day!' And we're swiping, swiping . . ."

"Phase Thirty-Seven: Absolute Ban on Photos Where You Give the Peace Sign."

Azrael snored. Vexy and Hackus were bored.

"Phase Thirty-Eight: Absolute Ban on Fist Bumping and High Fives." There were two more slides. "Finally! Phase Thirty-Nine!" Gargamel raised the tablet and proclaimed the most ultimate phase of his plan. "Phase Thirty-Nine: Absolute Power and World Adulation."

The picture on the screen was of Gargamel at a Taj Mahal–type palace with hundreds of thousands bowing to him.

"Ahhh, yes, then I'll have enough essence to rule the world. Not to mention—Phase Forty!"

Gargamel swiped the screen one last time for the other most ultimate phase of his ultimate plan. "Phase Forty: Total Destruction of Smurf Village."

Gargamel turned the tablet toward his sleeping cat. The picture was of the Smurfs' mushroom village. The town was completely destroyed. "Oh, how it warms the cockles." Gargamel sniffed back happy tears. "I'm sorry. I always get a little emotional at this part."

Overcome with joy, Gargamel put his head against the screen.

Azrael woke up. "Meow."

"I'm wasting time? You sleep eighteen hours a day and lick yourself the other six."

Azrael reached across Gargamel and swiped the slides back to Phase 2, with the Eiffel Tower.

"Right." Gargamel reviewed the image. "The very reason we chose this resplendent metropolis: the great iron antenna. The only way to harness enough energy to create a portal right into Smurf Village."

Gargamel picked up his dragon wand and stood. "Let us away!"

"Father. Wait!" Vexy called out.

Gargamel turned to find that Vexy and Hackus had grown pale and weak.

"Oh. Yes, of course. More mouths to feed." From the vial around his neck, Gargamel dripped tiny drops of essence onto each of their little tongues.

The Naughties instantly felt better. Gargamel poured the last bit of the essence into his dragon wand.

"Now." He pointed the wand toward the penthouse door. "To the antenna!"

KABOOOM! Gargamel waved the wand to create thunder and lightning above the Eiffel Tower.

"ALAKAZAMM!"

Lightning struck the tower. One large fiery bolt hit a coil, becoming a tight laser of energy shooting over the Seine River and electrifying the reflecting pools of the Trocadero.

KABOOOOM!

Electricity crackled throughout the water. A whirlpool began to form.

Gargamel checked his dragon wand.

"Perfect! Just enough essence!"

Gargamel flew across the river, toppling headfirst toward the whirlpool. Below the swirling water, there was a portal.

"Ready or not, here I—"

WHANG!

Gargamel's head got stuck in the portal. He spun around, like in a washing machine.

Azrael and the Naughties rushed to the edge. They couldn't help laughing.

When Gargamel managed to pull out his head, his hair and eyebrows stood straight up.

"Seems I lacked sufficient essence for a human-size portal." He took the vial from his neck. It was empty.

"Meow."

"I have not put on weight!" Gargamel said, patting his belly. "Maybe a couple of pounds. It's those croissants!"

"Father, I can fit through there," Vexy said.

"Hackus go! Hackus go!" Hackus begged.

"Well, let's see. Eeny, meeny, miney . . ." Gargamel's finger pointed to Hackus. "Moron."

"No!" Vexy stomped on Hackus's foot and popped his ears. Then Vexy leaped into Gargamel's hand. "I win."

Gargamel nodded. "Nicely played. Now I must warn you, your destination is a horror, a realm filled with the relentless, crushing quiet, punctuated by the wretched cacophony of joyousness and a monstrously repetitive song."

Vexy shivered.

"Exactly," Gargamel said. "It ruined your sister."

"I hate her," Vexy said.

"That's the spirit! That annoyingly perky Smurfette is a turncoat and an ingrate! That ridiculous little Papa Smurf brainwashed her and turned her against me. Me? Of all people?" Gargamel groaned in disbelief.

"Poor Father," Vexy said. "It's such a shame when evil is corrupted by good."

"So true," Gargamel replied. "But she knows the secret formula. So go and get her." With all his wizard strength, Gargamel threw Vexy into the portal.

Chapter 5

Smurfette walked along the bank of the Smurf Village pond.

"I just don't get it. They know how tough my birthday can be, and they didn't even remember." She sat down at the water's edge and looked at her reflection. "Guess I'll never really be one of them."

Suddenly, Vexy rose through the watery reflection.

"Ahhhh!" Smurfette stood up and began to run.

"Please. Help. I escaped."

"Escaped?" Smurfette turned back to see Vexy climbing out of the water.

Vexy was out of breath and panting. Leaning her hands on her knees, she choked out, "From the evil wizard who made me."

Smurfette stepped closer. "Do you mean Gargamel? Did Gargamel make you?!"

Vexy nodded.

"But he's . . ." Smurfette's eyes went wide with shock. "That means you're just like me." Smurfette rushed to her. But the instant she got near enough, Vexy grabbed her around the waist.

"Gotcha!"

Smurfette struggled to break free. "What are you doing?"

Vexy dragged her toward the water. "Father is gonna be very happy."

In a panic, Smurfette began to shout. "Help! Heeeelp! Code Red!"

Handy Smurf heard the yell. He dropped his hammer. "Smurfette's in trouble!"

The Smurfs rushed down the pathway to the pond.

"She's being smurfnapped!" Greedy said as he reached the portal's edge.

Hefty shouted out, "Smurfette!"

With a wicked grin, Vexy shoved Smurfette through the mist. "So long, Smurrrrrrrfs!"

"NOOOOOOO!" Gutsy and the others charged the portal, but it closed before they could jump through.

Brainy shook his head. "It doesn't take a genius to tell you, but I will: This is the work of Gargamel!"

In France, the swirling whirlpool-portal coughed up Smurfette and Vexy. Gargamel grabbed Smurfette, tightening his fist around her waist. "Ah, the Smurfette. Welcome home."

Azrael glared at Smurfette, revenge in his cat eyes.

Smurfette was scared. And her fear grew when Gargamel began to laugh.

Chapter 6

In New York City, Patrick and Grace Winslow were having a party for their son's third birthday.

Patrick set the cake on the table. "Here you go, Blue." He glanced around at the guests. "I think I have everyone's issues covered. It's an organic, gluten-free, antioxidant-rich, sustainably grown acai-berry cake with fair-trade, nondairy vanilla icing, all made locally by a cruelty-free baker who swears he's never even seen a peanut. Everyone's good, right?"

Carolina, a friend of Grace's asked, "Are the plates PCB-free?"

"Wrong!" Patrick headed to back into the kitchen to see what other dishes they might have.

"Actually, we're good." Grace showed Carolina the wrapper's label.

"We're good! You see that, guys?" Patrick happily

pointed at the package. "PCB and BPA free. There are virtually no letters in these plates." Patrick slipped an arm around Grace. "Boy, who ever thought parenting would be so complicated?"

"Seriously?" a father asked. "'Cause you guys almost make it look easy."

Henri, another parent, said, "You know Patrick. I'm sure he read every book on fatherhood ever written."

Henri's wife, Vanessa, added, "You must've had a great role model."

Patrick frowned. "Me? Oh, um, not really. My dad left when I was five. So the only 'role' he ever 'modeled' was the one where you quietly 'roll' the car out of the driveway and never come back." Patrick waited for a laugh—but all the other parents just stared at him.

Patrick shrugged. "What? No fans of abandonment humor?"

The front door banged open. Victor Doyle thumped his way into the room.

"Am I late?" Victor's hair was a mess and his clothes rumpled, as if he'd just woken up. "Did I miss the presents? All week I've been tryin' to sort out what to get Blue. A toy? A game? A ball? Somethin' electriclike? Then I said to myself, 'What are you talking about? Get him everything!'" Victor grabbed a rope and tugged a red wagon piled high with presents in from the hallway.

He wheeled the wagon near Blue, then kissed the boy on the head.

"Grampa Vicster!" Blue cheered.

"Blue!" Victor scooped his grandson into a bear hug. "Happy birthday, Blue. That's right. Now it's a party!"

A woman leaned in toward Patrick and whispered, "Who's he?"

Victor set Blue down at the table. "I'm Victor, Patrick's dad. And you must all be his friends. Which makes you my friends. So, let's go. Everybody up. Arms in the air. You're all gettin' hugs!"

One of the parents broke free of Victor's tight embrace and asked Patrick, "I thought you said your father left you."

Patrick watched Victor work his way around the room. "He did. Which paved the way for him . . . my stepfather."

Patrick pulled Grace aside. "What is he doing here?"

Grace replied, "It's Blue's birthday. I invited him."

Patrick moved out of the way just in time. "There's my Gracie. Come here, darlin'." Victor barreled forward and swept Grace into his arms. "Ever since Blue was born, I kinda miss you being big as a house. There was more of you to hug."

Victor raised his voice over the other parents' chatter. He had an announcement. "Let me tell you something. This woman right here is a saint. She's kind, brilliant, generous, and she does a mean booty-bump!"

On cue, Victor and Grace turned sideways to bump booties. The impact sent Grace flying across the room.

"Sorry, I forget we're in different weight classes." Victor went to help her up.

Victor announced, "And now I saved the biggest hug for last." Patrick took a couple of steps back. Victor matched his steps by moving forward. "C'mon, son. Let's show 'em how it's done."

Patrick pointed at Victor. "Boundaries, remember. Boundaries!"

With a giant swoop, Victor lifted Patrick off the ground and held him tight. "Ug-ug-ug-ug." He bounced Patrick up and down.

"Don't—like—this—at—all," Patrick stammered breathlessly between bounces.

"Ahh, yeah, there's nothing like an embrace between two proud Doyle men," Victor said.

"I am not a Doyle man," Patrick replied.

Victor set Patrick on the ground, then ruffled his hair. "Actually—you are. I legally changed your name when you were eleven, remember?"

"Without telling me. And I changed it back when I was eighteen," Patrick said.

"Without telling me?" Victor raised an eyebrow.

"Well, aren't you the sneaky one, Paddy Doyle?"

"Winslow," Patrick said.

Victor countered, "Doyle."

"Winslow," Patrick repeated.

Victor gave in. "All right. A compromise. Winslow-hyphen-Doyle." As he said it, Victor coughed.

Vanessa suddenly recognized Victor. "Hey, isn't he the guy from those corn dog commercials on TV?"

Patrick tried to stop the conversation. "No, no."

But another mother said, "Hey, you're right!"

Victor's face beamed as he said, "Well, you got me. Guilty as charged."

Patrick was so mortified that he wanted to disappear. "Here we go . . ."

Victor pulled out a thermal bag with his distinct logo. "The Korndog King! Always remember, regular corn dogs are spelled with a *C*. Mine are spelled with a *K*—for 'kwality'—that's how you know they're better."

Patrick leaned over to Grace. "See, this is exactly what he does."

Victor raised his arms. "And now, in honor of Blue's birthday, I'm going to distribute to each one of you a free korndog. On the house. But don't get it 'on the house.' I just made that up. Look for it in the next commercial."

Patrick covered his eyes with his hands as Victor went up to each guest, offering them a korndog.

"All right now—nobody say a word! I am an expert at matching the right face with the right dog." He approached an Italian friend. "Garlic and cheese—*buon appetito*!"

To the Japanese couple, he said, "Teriyaki dog. *Kampai, ichiban*!"

"Barbecue pork for my homey," Victor tells Henri, passing the stick.

"Oh my god." Patrick was humiliated.

Patrick felt like he was going to die of embarrassment. "Perfect. If you can't be sensitive, just offend everyone."

Victor laughed. "Ooookay, everyone has their insult? Nobody's left out?"

Carolina asked, "Do these have any peanuts?"

"What? I would never put peanuts in a corn dog," Victor answered.

"Great."

Carolina nodded to her son that it was okay to take a bite, when Victor said, "We fry them in peanut oil."

"What?!" Carolina grabbed the dog from her son, but it was too late. Her husband dove for the diaper bag to get an allergy shot.

Patrick dropped his head into his hands.

Victor didn't understand. "What's happening to that kid's lips?"

Chapter 7

Gargamel dragged Smurfette back to his hotel suite. Smurfette was terrified, but acted brave.

"You're wasting your time, Gargamel," she told him. "Papa and the others are gonna come for me."

"I don't think so," Gargamel said.

"They came for Clumsy." Smurfette reminded him of the last time he tried to capture the Smurfs.

"Yes, but you see, Clumsy was a real Smurf." Gargamel's words cut Smurfette, like a sharp knife to her heart. Smurfette held back her tears.

"I was the one who made you, Smurfette. Darling daughter." He stepped away from her.

Smurfette turned her sadness and fear into anger. "You're not my father. Just let go!"

"Smurfette, if you want to go 'home,' all I need you to do is one little, tiny, itsy-bitsy favor."

"What?" She *did* want to go home.

"Just give me the secret formula that Papa used to turn you into a Smurf."

Smurfette was stunned.

Hackus was excited at the thought of becoming a Smurf. "Hackus blue! Hackus blue!"

Gargamel ignored Hackus and said to Smurfette, "Don't you see, my dear. It would benefit us both. You give me the formula. I turn my Naughties blue. I use their essence to continue doing my humble yet wildly successful magic show here. And then I'll never again have to bother you or the rest of that unbelievably annoying Smurf Village that you seem to love so much for some unfathomable reason."

"I don't believe you," Smurfette said.

Gargamel smiled. "Why not? I love it here." He turned to Hackus and Vexy and asked, "Don't I love it here?"

They nodded.

He turned back to Smurfette. "The people of this realm adore me. They think—and this is them talking—that I'm the greatest sorcerer they've ever seen. Always clapping and cheering and bowing." Gargamel quickly added, "Completely unsolicited, by the way."

Smurfette shook her head. "I don't trust you. I'm not telling you anything."

"I see. Well, perhaps you just need a little persuasion."

The wizard pointed at his creations and then at Smurfette. "Naughties . . . attack!"

Hackus attacked Vexy.

"Not each *other*!" Gargamel shouted in frustration.

They went after Azrael.

"Not the cat! Not the lamp, either!"

"Meow," Azrael said, watching the Naughties move around the room, leaping from thing to thing.

"Deeply, deeply disappointing experiments." Gargamel sighed.

Back at Smurf Village, Papa Smurf's mushroom was crowded with Smurfs.

"All right, Smurfs, listen up." Papa called the meeting to attention. "I saved some grotto water from the last Blue Moon for just such an occasion. I was able to smurf it into smurfportation crystals."

"So we don't need a portal?" Brainy was impressed. "Very clever, Papa."

"Smurfzactly." Papa showed them all the crystals. "These will take us directly to Master Winslow's apartment mushroom. If anyone can help us, it's he and Miss Grace."

Clueless Smurf looked around the room. "Are we having a birthday party for Smurfette?"

They all ignored him.

Blue hands shot up into the air. All the Smurfs wanted to volunteer to go on the mission.

"Now, now, Smurfs. I only had enough grotto water for nine crystals. That's me and three others, round trip, plus Smurfette on the way home," Papa explained.

Grouchy grumped. "Assuming you can find her—which is doubtful."

"That's not a very smurfy attitude, Grouchy," Clumsy said.

"Actually, for me, that was pretty good," Grouchy replied.

Papa searched the volunteers. "I'll need courage, strength, and intelligence. So . . . Gutsy, Hefty, Brainy—you'll smurf with me." He called on a Smurf with a question. "Yes, Passive-Aggressive Smurf?"

"I just wanna say I think Brainy is a really excellent choice. Good luck with that." Passive-Aggressive Smurf snickered.

"See what he does? Why doesn't that feel like a compliment?" Brainy frowned.

Papa crossed the room to Hefty and gave him some crystals.

At the same time, Clumsy went to congratulate the three chosen Smurfs. "Go get her, guys! We know you can—" As he spoke, Clumsy tripped over his own feet and knocked into Papa. Most of the crystals tumbled to the floor, except for three. Those few crystals flew out of Papa's hand and landed into Hefty's mouth.

"Oops." Clumsy was horrified by what he'd done.

Hefty began to choke, holding his throat, gasping for breath.

"Oh no! He can't breathe!" Panicky exclaimed. "He's gonna die! We're all gonna die! Ahhh!"

Gutsy said, "Stand back. I know the Smurflich maneuver." He jumped behind Hefty and wrapped his arms around the Smurf's chest.

"Oh dear, he's turning bluer!" Vanity exclaimed.

"This is going even worse than I thought it wou—" Grouchy began when suddenly—*UMPF!* The crystals came shooting out of Hefty. They soared through the air, straight into the open mouths of Grouchy, Clumsy, and Vanity.

"Oh no!" Clumsy said.

"I get so puffy when I travel!" Vanity tried to cough up the crystal.

"A pill on an empty stomach! I'm going to get sick," Grouchy complained.

Lazy Smurf had some advice. "Okay, three simple rules for safe travel. One . . ."

The others leaned in, eager for the safety tips, but Lazy slid into a deep, snoring sleep before he finished his thought.

POP! POP! POP!

All at once, Clumsy, Vanity, and Grouchy disappeared from Papa's mushroom. All that remained of the three traveling Smurfs was Vanity's mirror, laying on the floor.

Passive-Aggressive Smurf looked at the mirror and said, "Papa, I'm sure Narcissism, Ineptitude, and Pessimism will be just as helpful. Good luck with that."

"Why, thank you, Passive-Aggressive Smurf. I think. Well . . ." Papa picked up his last two crystals from the ground. He stuffed one in his satchel and put the other in his mouth. "Smurf us luck."

When they were gone, Brainy turned to the rest of the Smurfs. "By my calculation, they've got a point-oh-oh-oh-three chance of success."

Clueless turned to him and asked, "So, wait, we *are* having a party for Smurfette?"

Blue's birthday party was over. The guests had all left.

Patrick was on the phone, checking on the boy with the peanut allergy. "Well, I'm glad his throat opened up and his lips are back to normal and the red splotches are gone and he can see again. Great! And how was the ambulance ride? That is fantastic—and again, we're very sorry." He hung up and turned to Victor. "So, Tyler can breathe again—which makes two of us since his parents are both lawyers."

"So that's why they overreacted," Victor said.

Patrick was very mad. "They didn't overre—"

Victor wasn't paying attention. He looked at Blue and said, "I think he's ready for this." He reached over to Blue and raised a plastic Korndog King crown over his grandson's head.

"Don't put the crown on him," Patrick protested.

"You loved this crown," Victor replied, looking at the plastic ring.

"No. I didn't," Patrick said.

"You wore it everywhere," Victor reminded him.

"Never did."

Just then Blue began to flap his arms wildly.

Victor turned to the boy. "No, Blue! What are you doing? How many times have I gotta tell you?" He moved the boy's hand into position. "You gotta do it like this—from the armpit!"

Victor showed Blue how to make rowdy fart noises with hands and pits.

Blue was so excited. While Victor and Blue perfected the noise, Patrick snuck away into the kitchen.

"Do you see what's going on out there?" he asked Grace.

"They're bonding," Grace said as she cleaned up.

Patrick looked out into the living room. Victor and Blue were playing another game. "Technically they're spitting." He was disgusted.

Grace laughed. "Honey, Blue needs to learn that family means more than just you and me. It's good for him to play with his grandfather."

"Stepgrandfather," Patrick corrected.

"Why are you so down on him?" Grace asked.

The fart noises from the other room had begun again.

Patrick groaned. "That ain't exactly gonna get him into Harvard, is it?"

"Come on, Patrick." Grace lovingly put her hand on his shoulder.

"Grace, he ruins everything. That's his gift. Ruining things. Like when he first moved in with me and Mom and sent my parrot away." Patrick had a headache.

"Your parrot?" Grace asked.

"My father's parrot," Patrick explained. "When my dad took off, it was the only thing he left behind. I loved that bird. Used to ride around on my handlebars. Sleep on my headboard. But when Vic came, we had to get rid of him. 'Cause Vic was allergic."

Grace was about to reply when a new sound came from the other room.

WOOOMF, WOOOMF, WOOOMF.

"A helicopter?" Grace asked.

Patrick ran to the window to check.

Victor and Blue heard the noise as well. Blue covered his ears as the sharp sound grew louder and louder. Suddenly—*BOOOOOOM!*

A small blue comet crashed into Blue's pile of birthday gifts.

Patrick and Grace tried to shove open the door between the kitchen and the living room, but it wouldn't budge. Air pressure was holding it shut.

Patrick shouted to Victor. "DO YOU HAVE BLUE?!"

"Ahhhhhh!" Victor began to scream as a big plushy corn dog emerged from the pile of gifts and began to waddle toward him.

"I'm blind! I'm blind!" the corn dog shrieked.

Grace called out from the kitchen. "Victor! We can't open the door!"

Patrick slammed into the door repeatedly, trying desperately to shake the hinges.

In the living room, Victor grabbed a toddler chair. He was going to fight off the waddling corn dog when another loud sound exploded and a second blue comet fell to the floor.

This little blue monster smashed into Victor's face, clinging to him like an octopus. Victor fell backward onto the floor.

Clumsy Smurf sat on the old man's chest, staring at Victor, eyeball to eyeball.

"Sorry. I was smurfin' for the pillows, but your face got in the way," Clumsy explained with a shrug.

Patrick and Grace recognized the voice from behind the door.

"Clumsy?!" Patrick shouted through the stuck wood.

Victor swiped at Clumsy, attacking him when the third comet crashed.

BOOM!

This one landed between the coats on the hanging rack.

"Where am I?" Vanity Smurf was freaking out. "This place is strange! And terrifying! And"—he caught a glimpse of himself in the little mirror on the rack—"sooo handsome." Vanity calmed down and grinned. "Hello, you!"

BOOM!

The final blue comet landed in the thermal Korndog sack. Papa rolled out of the bag with a corn dog stuck in his hat.

"Did it work?" Papa asked, looking around, searching for his Smurfs.

"No! We're in the abyss! I knew it would end like this!" Grouchy was still stuck inside the stuffed corn dog toy. He stumbled forward.

"Watch out!" Clumsy warned.

Victor was armed with a weapon. Waving a plastic light saber, he swung toward Papa. Papa leaped out of the way in time, but the saber hit the corn dog plush toy, knocking it off Grouchy.

"Oh. This isn't the abyss," Grouchy said, very relieved.

The air pressure in the apartment returned to normal. The kitchen door flew open. Patrick and Grace tumbled into the room just as Victor was about to take a batter's swing at Grouchy's head.

"Victor! Stop! They're friends!" Patrick threw himself into the saber's pathway.

Victor refused to lower his weapon. "Friends?! They're little blue aliens, tryin' to steal our faces!"

Vanity was insulted. "Little? I'm as high as three apples and twice as polished!" He grinned widely, showing his glimmering teeth.

"No. They're called Smurfs." Patrick took the saber from Victor and set it down.

Grace lifted Grouchy into her arms. "And they're the sweetest things you'll ever meet."

"Not me," Grouchy said.

Grace smiled and gave him a hug. "No. Not you, Grouchy."

Patrick bent down to greet his visitors. "Papa, Clumsy. How are you guys?"

"Smurfs! Smurfs! Smurfs!" Blue began to chant and dance around the room.

"That's right, Blue," Patrick told him. "These are the Smurfs we've told you about."

Victor trusted his grandson. "If Blue likes the Smurfs, then the Vicster likes the Smurfs."

Papa Smurf couldn't believe his eyes. "Oh my Smurf. Is that Blue?"

"He's huge!" Clumsy said, checking out the kid.

"I wouldn't want to be the stork that brought that guy," Grouchy added.

"Glad to see you are raising him smurfy!" Papa told Patrick.

While Papa and the others got to know Blue, Grace turned to Vanity. "And who is this handsome fellow?"

Vanity puffed out his chest. "I ask myself that every day." From under his hat, Vanity took out his small travel-size mirror and glanced at himself.

"That's Vanity," Papa told her.

"The pleasure's all yours." Vanity held out his hand for a shake.

"Little help over here!" Grouchy called from across the room.

Everyone looked over to find Blue shoving Grouchy into his armpit, pumping for the raspberry noise.

"Blue! No!" Grace grabbed Grouchy and took him

to safety. "Grouchy is not a whoopee cushion!"

Patrick gently explained, "Don't squeeze Grouchy; you don't know what will come out."

Blue made an icky face. "He smells funny."

Grouchy sniffed himself and agreed. "Yeah, I had a couple of extra Smurfberries for breakfast."

Patrick asked Papa, "So what are you guys doing here?"

Papa's face turned serious. "Smurfette's been taken!"

"What?" Grace asked. "What do you mean 'taken'?"

Vanity told her, "Snatched away by Gargamel."

"If we can find him, we'll find her," Papa said.

"Well, that won't be hard. He's a big star now. In Paris," Patrick explained.

Grace stepped toward the bedroom. "I'll start packing. Honey, get Blue's passport."

Victor was excited. "Yes! A rescue mission. I'll come too. You'll need all the help you can get."

"Whoa, whoa. Wait! Blue's passport?" Patrick tried to slow everyone down a beat.

"Honey, we can't just up and go to Paris." He tipped his head toward Victor. "Especially not all of us."

Grace put it to a vote. "All right, that's one no. Who votes yes?"

Everybody else raised their hand, even Blue.

"Daddy always loses." Blue giggled.

"This is my Smurfette we're talking about. We have to go," Grace told Patrick.

Patrick let it all sink in. He nodded. They'd all go. Blue too. Even Victor.

"If we're going to be traveling," Vanity said, "then we must sing the ancient traveling song for the safe return of the Smurfs. It is a song that requires multilayered harmonies and chord construction few humans have ever heard. Let's make sure we do this properly."

Papa Smurf considered what Vanity was saying. "Now. Let us honor those who came before us."

All the Smurfs begin to sing the La La song.

Patrick covered his ears.

Chapter 8

Grace, Victor, and Blue arrived in Paris, France. Patrick hailed a taxi to take them from the airport to their hotel.

"All right," he whispered to the Smurfs as the cab driver unloaded the bags. "We're all clear on the plan, right? We'll head over to Gargamel's show, see if Smurfette is there."

Grace had discovered a newspaper article about the wizard. The photo showed him standing in front of a fancy hotel.

"And I'll go to the Plaza Athénée and find out which room he's staying in. Victor, you and Blue can check into our room here."

"I—I—I was thinking . . . ," Victor began.

Patrick shut him down. "No 'I—I—I was,' Vic. That's the deal." He settled back in the taxi and told the cab driver, "Le Opera House, s'il vous plaît." Patrick raised an eyebrow to Grace and said, "My French is *très* sexeee, no?"

Grace leaned in through the cab's open window. "Maybe I should get you a beret?"

Patrick winked. "You can't handle me in a beret."

Grace snorted. "Oh, really? Is that what you think?"

Patrick and Grace were face-to-face, rubbing noses, when Grouchy popped his head out of Patrick's jacket, saying, "Hey! Get a 'shroom!"

Patrick stuffed Grouchy's head back into his coat with the other Smurfs.

The taxi pulled into traffic.

Smurfette was tied to a desk lamp in Gargamel's theater dressing room.

The La La song was playing on Gargamel's tablet. On the screen was a classic hypnotic swirl image. Gargamel held the screen close to Smurfette's face.

"Giiiiiiiiiiiive hiiim the forrrrrmula. Yooooou wannnnnt to giiiiiive it to hiiimmmmm."

Smurfette stood with her arms crossed. The hypnotism wasn't working. The La La song stopped and the screen read "buffering."

"Awwg! Really?" he asked Smurfette. "You can just listen to this song indefinitely? How is it not driving you insane?"

To prove she could stand there all day, Smurfette

began to sing along. "La, la, la-la-la—"

Vexy and Hackus were squirming on the ground, hands to their ears.

"Make it stop! It burns!" Vexy begged.

Hackus really was hypnotized. His eyes swirled just before he passed out cold.

Azrael curled up in a corner, away from it all.

A voice announced the time. *"Cinq minutes."*

Gargamel gave up with Smurfette. "Ah, my public awaits. Once again I must go astound and confound the merry imbeciles."

"Meow," Azrael informed him.

"Out of essence?" Gargamel had forgotten.

"Meow." Azrael looked toward Smurfette.

Gargamel grabbed a pair of scissors. "Oh, we can still do the show because I've got all the essence I need right here, now, don't I?"

"When Papa gets here, you're gonna be sorry." Smurfette tried to dodge Gargamel's clippers.

"I told you, Smurfette. Your papa is not coming—because your papa is already here." He pointed to himself. "See? I'm your papa." Gargamel cut off a large chunk of Smurfette's hair.

Smurfette was horrified, but then she realized Gargamel had also accidentally cut the ropes that held her to the lamp.

"So either you can give your real papa the formula or you can spend the rest of your miserable existence being harvested in my new superpowered Smurfalator." Gargamel laughed his wicked laugh. "It's up to you, my dear. Your decision."

When he turned to face her, Gargamel discovered Smurfette was escaping.

"Oh, and Smurfette"—he set a glass vase upside down over her head, trapping her inside like a fly—"nice try."

Smurfette angrily pounded her fists against the glass.

"Meow."

"Don't be absurd," Gargamel told the cat. "Of course I won't let her go. Who am I? Sir Goody-Good of Two Shoes?" He giggled. "Ah yes. As soon as she gives up the secret, I'm going to toss her into the machine for a long life of pain, torture, and suffering."

"Meow."

"Yes, yes, I'll let you push the button," Gargamel promised.

The bell rang for the show to begin. Gargamel faced the Naughties. "Whilst I am gone, keep at her. Her brain has been washed. You must naughty it back up."

"Yes, Father," Vexy said.

"And if you see any other blue Smurfs about, take no chances. Spirit her back to the hotel immediately."

The Naughties agreed.

Gargamel told Azrael, "Eventually, that meddlesome Papa will arrive. He always does." He crossed to a wall in the dressing room and opened a secret panel. "And if she knows he's here, she'll feel loved and never divulge her secret. Yes, yes, we must break her soon."

Gargamel led the way out of the room through the panel and down a dark and winding staircase. "Now, come. We've essence to make."

Before leaving, Gargamel turned the La La song back on.

Hackus was about to stand up, but hearing the music—*BAAM!* He fainted again.

Smurfette watched Gargamel and Azrael disappear from the room. The hidden panel slipped back into place. Nearby, a mirror showed what Gargamel had done to her hair. He'd lopped one whole side away. Smurfette began to cry.

Grace stepped up to the fancy hotel's front desk. "Hi. I was wondering if you'd be so kind as to tell me—"

The clerk pointed at the door. "What room Monsieur Gargamel is in? No. Hotel policy."

Grace wasn't sure what to do next. But then she saw a flyer she hadn't noticed before. An Audrey Hepburn film festival was coming to Paris. That gave her an idea.

Patrick's taxi pulled up in front of the opera house. Tossing the fare at the driver, Patrick jumped out and ran up the main stairs, holding his coat tightly shut.

The theater was packed with people. Patrick entered just as the house lights began to dim. He slipped through a side exit and approached the stage.

"Mesdames et messieurs—Gargamel le Great!" an announcer opened the show.

The theater lights brightened. Thick fog filled the stage. Gargamel made his appearance.

"You call that a Shroud of Mystery?!" Gargamel was insulted there wasn't more fog. "A wisp, at best."

ZZAPP!

With a flick of the dragon wand, the fog grew heavier. Gargamel backed up, and to roaring applause, he stepped through it again.

He enjoyed the spotlight, then coughed a little.

"Good evening, unworthy admirers. I am Gargamel the Great. Tonight you will witness no trivial illusions, but rather the most spectacular genuine sorcery the world has ever seen! Some of you may die." The audience broke out into a fit of excited giggles. Gargamel paused. "Don't know why that always gets a laugh. The people of this realm are bewildering."

The wizard's voice boomed through the theater.

"But be warned! If any of your beeping, ringing contraptions should interrupt the demonstration of my amazing wizardry, or should I hear any crinkling noise from the shiny wrappings of your confectionery sweet meats . . . you'll all pay dearly."

Before the first trick, Gargamel warned the audience, "Now, in the event of a fire, and there usually is one, feel free to scream, panic, and trample one another like dogs. If my spectacle is to be disrupted, at least I should be amused."

While Gargamel was focused on his show, Patrick moved behind the curtain, backstage.

"A guard!" Patrick told the Smurfs to duck. He approached the guard. *"Parlez-vous Anglais?"*

"Non." The guard didn't speak any English.

"Great." Patrick could use it as his secret language. He whispered into his coat, "Okay, Papa. Sneak out of the back of my jacket while I'm talking to this man and find the dressing room."

The Smurfs slid down the back of Patrick's leg, scattering into the darkness.

Grace returned to Gargamel's hotel. She was dressed in high heels and a floppy hat.

"I am outraged! Outraged I tell you!" Grace smacked the countertop with her long black gloves.

That got the hotel clerk's attention. "I am sorry, who are you?"

"I am Monsieur Gargamel's manager, Madame . . . Doolittle. I've just returned from my Roman holiday, only to find my client greatly displeased with his accommodations. What is this . . . this outhouse you call a room?"

The clerk was surprised. "The Napoléon Suite? Madame, this is the finest room in all the hotel. What could possibly—"

Grace cut him off. "For one thing, it is on the wrong floor. Nobody wants to be on the . . . the . . ."

"The fifth floor," the clerk finished.

"Yes! That is too low!" Grace pretended to be insulted.

"But the fifth is our top floor," the clerk explained.

"Then build another!" Grace smacked her gloves against the counter again, and in a huff, strutted away.

"Oh boy," she whispered to herself as she rushed toward the elevators. The door opened and Grace got in, immediately pressing the number five. Nothing happened. The elevator didn't move. She pressed the floor number again.

The assistant manager for the hotel entered the elevator and asked, "Do you have your key card?"

Grace fumbled in her purse. "Yes, of course I have my key card. I am a very important guest!"

The assistant manager waited while she emptied her bag.

Grace pinched her lips together. "I just . . . left it. I was having breakfast . . . at Tiffany's . . . and I left it there. I'll go back and get it."

She hurried out the elevator. As the doors closed behind her, she noticed another way up. A nearby sign said: VESTIAIRE DES EMPLOYÉS—EMPLOYEE LOCKER ROOM.

Grace had another idea.

At the opera house, the Smurfs searched for Smurfette. They shimmied up the backstage ropes and made their way across the rigging.

"Oh my smurf! Look at that stage!" Vanity was entranced. "The curtains! The lights!" He couldn't stop himself. "I feel a song coming on. . . ." He found a prop nearby that looked like the mask from *The Phantom of the Opera*. He began a song from that show: "Smurfly, gently . . ."

Papa put his fingers to his lips. "Shhh."

Clumsy whispered, "What are you doing?"

Vanity replied, "What I was born to do!"

"This whole thing's gonna be a smurftastrophe," Grouchy predicted.

"Now why would you say that?" Papa asked.

"Our names are Grouchy and Clumsy." He nodded toward Vanity and said, "And he's got a flower behind his ear."

Clumsy was insulted. "Hey, I'm a hero. You just watch—" Just then Clumsy tripped and nearly fell off the rigging, barely catching himself in time.

Grouchy moaned. "No shame in giving up. Everyone, home."

Moving slowly, the Smurfs continued toward Gargamel's dressing room.

Azrael was sitting in the wings, watching the show. A familiar scent wafted by him, and he raised his head. He didn't usually interrupt Gargamel's performances, but this was important.

"All hail, as the great and exceedingly powerful Gargamel unleashes—"

"Meow," Azrael said.

"What are you doing out here? How dare you! If you have to make a boom-boom, your box is out back," Gargamel told the cat.

"Meow."

"You smell something suspicious? Of course you do. I've seen where you put your nose." Gargamel sneered. The audience laughed.

It wasn't a joke. "Stop that! Why do you chortle?"

A man in the front row explained, *"Le chat est petit!"*

"What?" Gargamel didn't speak French.

The man said, "Usually, in majeek—zee cats are very big, no? Lions. Tigers."

"You make a good point." Gargamel considered Azrael's size. "On the other hand . . . Silence, knaves!" He quieted the audience and then raised his wand. "If it is a big cat you crave, allow me to oblige . . . *ALAKAZANIMAL!*"

ZAPPP! POOF!

Azrael grew to twice the size of a tiger.

"ROOOOOAAAAARRRRR!"

For a moment, Gargamel was surprised at what he'd done to his cat. His magic was strong. But then his shock faded as the audience went wild, screaming his name and applauding. Gargamel basked in the glow of their praise.

Chapter 9

"We need to come up with some ingenious way to get Smurfette talking. Got any ideas?" Vexy paced the dressing room backstage at the opera house. She had her back to Smurfette, who was still trapped under the glass vase.

Hackus considered her question. "Uhhhhhhhhhhhhhhh . . ."

"Never mind. I forgot you were . . ." She stared at him, adding, "You." Vexy went on. "All right, here's my plan: We trick her into being naughty. Use all her goodness against her. Once that happens, she'll feel like one of us and then . . ."

While they discussed options, Smurfette managed to push the vase halfway off the countertop's edge. But before she could slip out, the container toppled. Glass shattered.

The Naughties looked up just in time to see

Smurfette escape through an air vent.

"Oh no. Get her!" Vexy grabbed Hackus and began to follow Smurfette.

On the stage, Gargamel was performing with the lion-size Azrael.

"Oh, come now," he said as a spotlight glided over the audience. "One volunteer to stick their head in the little kitty's mouth. He just ate. There's a very good chance you'll survive. At the very worst, lose an ear or get a bad haircut. Anyone?"

The spotlight continued to travel from face to face while Gargamel searched for a volunteer.

Patrick ducked as the light passed near his hiding place. "Oof." He bumped into someone. Patrick turned around to discover it was Victor.

Victor whispered, "Hey, how's it going?"

Blue was with him.

Patrick was surprised. "Blue! How did you—"

Blue was standing in the shadows eating a crepe filled with chocolate and licking his lips.

"Yeah, yeah, yeah. Listen, Blue and I couldn't let you roll solo on this. I know you and I have had our differences, but when we face danger, we're all Americans," Victor explained.

Patrick raised an eyebrow. "What does that even mean?"

Victor pointed at Blue. "Three generations of proud Doyle men, standing shoulder to shoulder—even though we're all different heights and what not."

Patrick groaned. "We are not Doyle men."

Victor refused to argue. "Winslow-hyphen-Doyle. You got a real bee in your bonnet about the whole name thing."

Patrick searched for the nearest exit. "You have to go."

"After we get the Smurfette girl," Victor said.

Before Patrick could stop him, Victor stepped into the aisle.

Onstage, Gargamel was saying, "Trust me, eventually he coughs up everything he eats."

"Yo! Magic man!" Victor marched down the aisle. The spotlight moved to follow him. "Hand over the Smurfette."

Gargamel squinted into the light. "You—what did you say?"

"Are you deaf?" Victor was getting closer to the stage. "You heard me. Give me the Smurfette. Now!"

"Who are you? How dare you!" Gargamel raised his wand. *"ALAKAZ—"*

"DUCK!" Patrick leaped from his hiding place.

"Duck!" Gargamel repeated. The blue flame shot out of Gargamel's wand. "Duck?"

ZZZZAP!

The wizard's magic turned Victor into a duck.

"Uh-oh. I'm a duck and I'm in France," Victor quacked nervously. "I don't like where this is headed."

The audience applauded for the trick.

"NO!" Patrick shouted as the spotlight found him.

"Great Merlin's beard! I remember you!" Gargamel exclaimed.

Patrick quickly turned. He had to protect Blue.

ZAP!

It was too late. Patrick began to levitate up over the crowd.

"Daddy can fly!" Blue shrieked in delight. "Daddy can fly! Go, Daddy! Go!"

"Love you, son!" Patrick called to Blue, pretending this was all part of his plan.

Gargamel chuckled. "It appears we have a volunteer after all, ladies and gentlemen."

He used the blue flame to drag Patrick to the stage. "Open wide, Azrael."

"Roar!" Azrael opened his mouth as his meal soared over the cheering crowd.

The Smurfs tumbled into Gargamel's dressing room through an open window. Clumsy landed and immediately busted into his best kung-fu moves. His hands and feet were flying everywhere.

"Who-ya! Ki-waka!" Clumsy kicked too high. His feet flew out, and he crashed onto his back. "Oooof."

"Good work, Clumsy," Grouchy said. "You just lost a fight to an empty room."

While the Smurfs searched around for Smurfette, Patrick was about to be fed to Azrael.

"Put him down!" Victor the Duck came flying toward Gargamel, wings flapping. He flew into Gargamel's face, breaking his energy beam's hold on Patrick.

Patrick crashed onto the stage.

"Roar!" As Azrael was about to gobble up Patrick, Victor bumped into Gargamel's wand. An accidental blast transformed Azrael back to normal size.

"Cursed duck!" Gargamel turned his wand toward Victor.

Patrick boldly grabbed Victor and dove off the stage. With a speedy swoop, Patrick picked up Blue and dodged Gargamel's wand's blasts as he led them all safely out the exit.

The audience thought what they had just seen was

part of the show. They stood to clap as they whooped and hollered for Gargamel. The applause shook the house.

"Uh . . . and that's all the show we have time for today. Good-bye!" Gargamel bowed then hurried away.

In Gargamel's dressing room, the Smurfs made an important discovery.

"There's some sort of hidden passage here." Grouchy called everyone around to see the secret panel.

Papa helped Grouchy slide it open. Spiral stairs led down into darkness.

"Rage before beauty." Vanity stepped back to make way for Grouchy.

Clumsy stepped onto a table. Accidentally, he turned on Gargamel's tablet. The first picture on the screen was of the wizard.

"Ahhh!" Clumsy screamed as he tripped. The tablet fell to the ground.

Everyone cautiously approached the device.

"It's some sort of magic window." Footsteps in the hallway made Papa look up. "Quickly, Smurfs. Hide it."

Grabbing the tablet, the Smurfs hurried through the secret panel and down the stairs. The trapdoor closed behind them.

As the Smurfs rushed down the steps, they could hear

Gargamel's voice echoing above.

"Naughties? Smurfette? Where are you?! Your papa's back!"

"Her papa?" Clumsy whispered to the others.

Papa Smurf's face flushed red. *He* was Smurfette's Papa. But before he could say anything, the trapdoor opened and Gargamel shouted into the dark, "Are you down there?!"

The Smurfs stayed silent. Satisfied there was no one below, Gargamel slammed the door hard. The force of it made them all fall down the stairwell and into the lair below.

Above, Gargamel said, "They must have retreated to the hotel."

"Meow."

"Of course, we're running out of time! If Patrick of New Yorkshire is here . . . Papa can't be far behind."

Clumsy tapped the tablet, and the light from the screen made it easier to see. They were in the sewer under the opera house. Massive tunnels branched out in every direction. But here, in a large, open room, was a terrifying machine next to rows and rows of Smurf-size containers.

"Oh my smurf." Vanity stared at the tubes that led to a gigantic vat.

"It's a giant Smurfalator," Papa said. He'd once been attached to a smaller version of the machine.

"Why's it so big?" Grouchy asked.

"Guys." Clumsy had the answer. He held up the tablet. The screen read: "Phase 40: Total Destruction of Smurf Village."

An image of Smurf Village, smoldering in flames, flickered across the page. Not one single mushroom was left.

"Need a catch, please," Vanity said before he fainted backward into Grouchy's arms.

Outside the theater, Smurfette made her escape. The Naughties followed her into a narrow alleyway. Smurfette glanced over her shoulder at them, then ran faster.

Gargamel and Azrael left the opera house and headed to the hotel. When the wizard opened the stage door, a waiting crowd begged for autographs.

"Why is no one kneeling? Haven't we been over this, people?" Gargamel zapped them with his wand and they all fell to their knees at once.

Azrael looked to Gargamel.

"It doesn't mean as much if I have to keep doing it

myself. I want them to want to kneel," he said.

Azrael rolled his eyes as they climbed into the fancy carriage.

Someone was already inside, waiting. "Señor Gargamel."

Odile Anjelou, New York City's cosmetics queen, was sitting opposite Gargamel. Her long legs crossed elegantly in front of her.

"What are you doing here?" Gargamel glanced at her legs. "And why are you displaying your legs in this fashion?"

"Did you think you could escape to France and avoid me? We had a deal." She'd come all the way from New York to Paris.

"What deal? I have urgent matters to attend to. Be gone with you!" Gargamel put a hand on the carriage's door.

Odile wasn't leaving. "You promised to share your secret beauty formula with me. Remember?" She moved to sit next to him. "For one day, your incredible formula transformed my mother back into a ravishing beauty. Now my clients are all begging for it. Even my teenage daughter wants to try it." She reached forward to touch a small strand of Gargamel's hair. "And she's like me. She always gets what she wants."

Gargamel grabbed Odile's hand and shoved it away

from his head. “You have a stubborn, intractable daughter?”

“You have no idea.” Odile sighed.

“Suddenly you are of interest to me.” He raised his voice to the driver. “Onward, horseman! Giddyap, horseman!”

SMURFY CREEK
GROUCHY'S HOME
JOKEY'S HOME
SMURF VILLAGE MAIN SQUARE
PAPA'S HOME
VANITY'S HOME
MUSHROOM BRIDGE
SMURFETTE'S HOME
SMURF VILLAGE GARDEN
SMURF VILLAGE

Gargamel

Chapter 10

Patrick came out of the opera house holding Blue. Victor the Duck followed closely behind. Victor's feathers were ruffled, and chunks of food were stuck to his bill.

Patrick was angry. "We had a deal. Didn't we have a deal? You were going to watch Blue in the hotel."

"What are you so cross about? I'm the duck," Victor replied, flapping one wing.

"Because you're always barging in and ruining everything. You're like a walking disaster."

Victor stopped and gave Patrick the most serious look a duck could muster. "Look me in the eyes and say that."

"I can't." Patrick turned away.

"That's right. 'Cause it's not true," Victor said.

"No," Patrick told him. "It's because your eyes are on the sides of your head!"

"Ah! All the better for me to see your disrespect." Victor glared at him.

"Could you please hurry up?"

"Hey, I'm waddling as fast as I can, all right? Maybe if you laid out a trail of bread crumbs, I might be inclined to walk faster," Victor quacked.

When Patrick rounded the next corner, he found the Smurfs climbing out of a sewer grate.

"Papa! What happened?" Patrick hurried to them.

"We must find Smurfette quickly," Papa said. "Gargamel is hatching a terrible, terrible plan."

Grouchy noticed the big bird and asked, "What's with the duck?"

"No, that's Victor. Gargamel turned him into a giant duck," Patrick explained.

"Bad country to be walking around in as a duck." Grouchy looked up at Victor.

"That's what I said." Victor sighed.

A few blocks away, Smurfette was running down a small street. When she reached the intersection, she stopped. Paris was the most fabulous city Smurfette had ever seen. Shops, restaurants, people, scooters . . . She couldn't help but slow down to look around.

The Naughties easily caught up.

Vexy sent Hackus to a candy store, so she could talk to Smurfette alone. "Go get yourself in trouble. Even you can manage that."

"Trouble! Trouble! Hackus love trouble!"

When Hackus scurried away, Vexy approached Smurfette. "Hey, Blondie, where are you going?"

"Leave me alone," Smurfette replied.

"Aren't you tired of being alone?" Vexy asked. Her question made Smurfette frown. "I don't know how you did it, living in that village. I could never stay somewhere I didn't belong."

Smurfette raised her eyebrows and looked at Vexy.

"Look, Smurfette. I didn't kidnap you. I brought you home." Vexy waved her arms at the bustling streets.

Smurfette wondered if Vexy really did understand her. She was about to ask Vexy what she meant when the screaming began.

Across the street, Hackus was playing around in the candy store. Customers ran for safety as Hackus swung on a giant licorice rope, whipping himself around.

The candyman chased Hackus, but the small creature was fast. He popped a handful of gumballs into his mouth and began shooting them at the man.

Phoomp! Phoomp! Phoomp!

Hackus broke a glass jar of jawbreakers. They rolled all over the floor, tripping the escaping customers.

The candyman crashed into a heap.

Hackus flew backward into a bowl of nuts.

"Oooh! Right in the nuts," Hackus joked only to discover he was stuck in the bowl.

Vexy rushed into the candy shop. "Smurfette! He's gonna be killed! We have to help!"

"But . . ." Smurfette wasn't so sure.

Vexy rotated to face her. "I thought you were supposed to be good?"

Smurfette hesitated. Should she help the creatures who had kidnapped her? Could she trust them?

She decided she had to do what was right.

Smurfette went with Vexy into the candy shop.

The customers had left the store. The candyman and his assistant had Hackus cornered. The candyman was waving a large spatula. The assistant carried a frosting gun.

"Vexy!" Smurfette found a spoon on the counter. She climbed into the curvy end.

"Oooh, naughty!" Vexy jumped on the other end of the spoon, launching Smurfette into the air.

Smurfette landed on a jelly-filled donut. Direct hit! The jelly squirted into the candyman's eyes. Tripping backward, he crashed into some pans and trays.

Smurfette whirled a spatula at the assistant, causing him to accidentally point the frosting gun toward the candyman. The frosting hit the candyman in the face, and the two of them slammed into some shelves.

Smurfette grabbed Hackus, and they jumped onto a shopping cart.

"Nice move, stealing a cart!" Vexy cheered.

"I didn't steal it!" Smurfette protested.

"It's not yours, is it?" Vexy asked.

Hackus giggled. "Naughty, naughty, naughty!"

"See, maybe we're not so different after all," Vexy said.

Smurfette sat silently. She wasn't sure how to respond. Could Vexy be right?

Gargamel was riding in his carriage with Odile. "Tell me how you bend this horrible daughter of yours to your will."

Odile leaned in close. "As soon as you give me your secret formula."

"Look, if anyone is going to get a secret formula, it is I!" Gargamel said.

"What are you talking about?" Odile wasn't following the conversation.

Just then Azrael spotted the Naughties and Smurfette rolling out of the alley in the cart.

"Meow."

"Not now, Azrael," the wizard said.

"Meow!"

"Not now!" Gargamel smacked Azrael away.

"MEOW!" Azrael smacked Gargamel back with his paw.

"Not now!" Azrael and Gargamel began a slap fight.

To end it, Gargamel grabbed Azrael and threw him out the carriage window.

As the carriage continued through the streets of Paris, he said to Odile, "Now, back to your evil spawn."

The shopping cart with Smurfette and the Naughties flew out of the alley and hit a curb, sending the three of them tumbling into the mud.

"Yum, pudding." Hackus took a big drink of the goop.

"That's not pudding! It's mud," Smurfette told him.

"Yum, mud." Hackus licked his lips and slurped up some more.

Slipping out from the shadows, Azrael dove toward Smurfette and the Naughties.

They jumped out of the way as Azrael landed in the mud puddle with a splat.

With the cat right behind them, Smurfette led the

way through the alleys. At a fancy fountain, two French models, dressed like storks, were posing for a fashion shoot. The models were holding pretend babies while real live storks stood nearby.

"Quick! Get on the storks!" Smurfette showed Vexy how to jump onto the back of a bird.

Hackus jumped onto one of the models. "Hackus! Hackus! Hackus!" He kicked at her, trying to get the woman to lift off.

The model shouted for help and spun around, trying to knock Hackus from her back.

"Can you believe we're related to him?" Vexy asked.

Smurfette shrugged. "Well, it's nice to be related to someone." Then, louder, she called out, "No, Hackus! A real stork!"

Hackus jumped off the terrified model and onto a real stork and sat down—backward. The storks sailed into the sky.

The Naughties had never flown before.

"I can see forever!" Vexy exclaimed.

Hackus closed his eyes and said, "It's like flying!"

Smurfette laughed.

"Did you do this a lot back in Smurf Village with your sisters?" Vexy asked.

"Lots of flying. Never had a sister," Smurfette replied.

Vexy grinned. "Well, you've got one now!" Feeling

bold, Vexy swooped her stork down. Hackus's stork followed the skydive. "Hackus happy! Hackus happy!"

Seeing that he was still riding backward, Smurfette followed him. "Turn around! Before you get yourself killed!"

Hackus awkwardly rotated on the stork's back, barely missing a crash. "Oooooh!" He looked at the skyline below. "More like flying! Smurfette save Hackus! Hackus glad!"

"That's twice now," Vexy reminded Smurfette.

The three storks glided over the city. Smurfette noticed a mini Statue of Liberty.

"Wow! They've got these everywhere!" Smurfette said, recalling when she first visited New York City.

Odile and Gargamel were still in the carriage on the way to Gargamel's hotel.

"So, this daughter of yours is making you blue?" Odile asked him.

"No, no, no! She's not making anything blue. That's the problem." He clenched his teeth. "I've tried yelling, hypnosis, crushing her dreams, yet she remains unyielding. It makes me want to . . ." He stopped, considering what exactly he wanted to do.

"Cry?" Odile suggested.

"Flush her down the toilet," Gargamel said. "And soon her tiny, bearded stepfather will be here to ruin everything!"

Odile asked, "Have you tried kindness?"

"Kindness?" He didn't understand.

"Some praise, maybe. A gift? Even the most stubborn of us would respond to that. Don't you think?" Odile choked out a compliment for Gargamel. "My strappingly handsome genius?"

"Hmmm." Gargamel considered it. "Bribery and flattery to soften her stony heart. Counterintuitive, yes, but it just might work."

"Good. Now, your turn. What is the secret to staying beautiful?" She leaned in to hear his answer.

"You're a cunning wench and you've served me well. Allow me to express my heartfelt appreciation," Gargamel said.

He reached over and opened the carriage door, pushing Odile out into the street.

The carriage rolled away. Odile sat on the curb and muttered, "Why must all the geniuses be lunatics?"

Chapter 11

Patrick, Blue, and Victor met Grace in their hotel room.

"How'd it go?" Grace was still wearing her celebrity publicist costume.

"How do I think it went?" Grouchy complained. "I'm with Mr. Stumble-Bumble and Johnny Goodhair. Let's just say, it was a complete smurfwreck."

"No, it wasn't," Clumsy countered. "We didn't find Smurfette, but at least we know Gargamel's plan." Clumsy had brought the tablet from Gargamel's lair.

"He took her because she knows the secret to turning his fake, pale Smurfs blue," Patrick explained.

"He'd be able to make enough essence to rule the world," Papa told Grace.

"And obliterate Smurf Village." Vanity nearly fainted as he said it.

"It's the smurfin' smurfocalypse!" Grouchy said.

"But Smurfette would never tell him." Grace was certain.

"Never. Right, Papa?" Clumsy asked.

Papa's voice sounded a little concerned. "Uh . . . of course not. There's nothing to worry about there."

"Where's Vic?" Grace noticed he was missing.

"Oh, right." Patrick crossed to the window. "They wouldn't let him through the lobby, so he's flying up."

"Huh?" Grace followed him to the sill.

Patrick opened the window and Vic the Duck stepped inside.

"Hey, Gracie. Give us a hug, darlin'." When Victor raised his wings, a few feathers fell off.

Grace stepped away, shocked.

"Grampa Vicster is a duck!" Blue said, jumping.

"Gargamel zapped him," Patrick explained.

"Can you turn him back?" Grace asked Papa Smurf.

"It's a transformation spell," Papa told her. "It can only last so long."

"Everybody, relax. It's not a problem. But if you see me lay an egg, it's just between us." Victor sat on the couch.

"You don't seem very upset," Grace said to him.

"It's not in a duck's nature to get upset. We like to let things roll off our backs." Victor leaned forward and shook his feathers.

"Seriously? You actually said that?" Patrick stared at his stepfather.

"That's very smurfy of him," Papa said.

Victor quacked. "Thank you." Then to Patrick he said, "The little Santa Claus–Smurf appreciates me. Maybe someday you'll learn to appreciate my smurfy qualities too."

"I'm not having this conversation with a duck." Patrick sneezed. "And now I'm catching a cold."

"Of course you are!" Grouchy said. "Everything that can go wrong, will. It's Smurfy's Law!"

"Would you stop being so negative?" Clumsy was sick of it.

"I'm not negative. I'm just saying—" Grouchy was interrupted when Vanity held up a mirror in front of him. Grouchy went on. "We're in a hopeless situation we'll never get out of, and we're definitely gonna be miserable or dead for the rest of our lives!" He watched himself in the mirror, then remarked, "Holy smurf! I'm a downer!"

"Listen to me, Grouchy-fella," Victor told him. "Nobody ever accomplished anything positive by being negative. Okay?"

"That's a good one. I like that." Papa put a hand on Victor's shoulder.

"Good saying!" All the Smurfs agreed. "Very clever!"

"Thank you," Victor said. "I just made that up." He

tipped his beak. "What am I talking about? It's from a calendar I keep on my desk. I send one to Patrick every year, but he never lets on he gets them."

"That's not nice, Master Winslow," Papa said to Patrick. "You should thank people for gifts."

Patrick put his head in his hands.

"Hey, everybody, let's sing a song," Vanity said.

Victor joined in the La La song.

Patrick escaped to a corner with Grace. "How 'bout you? Any luck finding Gargamel's room?"

"Yeah," Grace said. "He's on the fifth floor. In the Napoléon Suite. And here's the good news." She was very proud of what she'd done. "I borrowed a waiter's outfit for you—complete with a security card for the elevator."

"How'd you manage that?" Patrick was impressed.

"The Plaza Athénée laundry room was paid a little visit by Audrey Hepburn's granddaughter, international apparel inspector." She gave herself a French accent. "Mademoiselle Doolittle!"

"Huh?" Patrick's jaw dropped.

"I'm, like, smurfin' Meryl Streep." Grace grinned widely.

Papa moved to the window and looked out on the large, sprawling city below. "I hope our Smurfette's okay."

Smurfette and the Naughties flew over the city. After everything that had happened that day, they were having a blast.

Hackus was having so much fun, he nearly fell off the stork.

Smurfette leaped onto his bird and set Hackus straight on it.

He hugged her tight. "Smurfette soft."

From her own stork, Vexy challenged, "Hey, you wanna race?"

"That depends. You wanna lose?" Smurfette's stork picked up speed.

"Oh, it's on!" Vexy swooped past.

"Hold on tight," Smurfette told Hackus.

He tightened his arms around her. "Okay."

The girls chased each other through Paris, sightseeing at the same time. They sped through an ice-cream parlor, dipped beneath the city's famous fountains, and even flew through the city's top fashion boutiques. Everyone had fun, even Hackus, though he may have gotten ice-cream–coned, splashed, and beskirted in the process!

At the outdoor market, Gargamel hurried down the sidewalk. "Kindness . . . gifts . . ." He was going to take

Odile's advice and buy a present for Smurfette.

"Du chocolat pour votre fille?" A woman offered to sell him chocolates.

"Out of my way, hag!" Gargamel pushed past. He muttered to himself, "Kindness . . . kindness . . ."

"Des fleurs, monsieur?" A young girl was selling beautiful flowers. She moved aside to show Gargamel the blossoms.

"Aww, what a delightful, gibberish-blathering urchin." He shoved her out of his way. "Can't you see I'm thinking of kindness?! You meddlesome little troll!"

His eyes wandered from stall to stall, looking for the right gift.

"What the devil does one give to express kindness?!" Gargamel muttered. Suddenly, he saw it. The present he needed. Perfect.

"Ahhh. What young woman's heart wouldn't be won by that?" Gargamel entered the shop to buy a Gargamania Junior Magic Kit, complete with a Gargamel action figure and junior wand.

Patrick was putting on the waiter's uniform. "He had no business being there," Patrick told Grace. He glanced out the bedroom door, but couldn't see Victor.

"He was just trying to help," Grace said.

"Getting turned into a duck is not a help. And why are you taking his side?" Patrick was having trouble with his bow tie.

"Look, Patrick, I grew up in northern Canada. I didn't have a relative for a thousand miles. I used to make pretend brothers and sisters out of snow. Then every spring I had to watch my extended family melt." She tied the tie for him.

Patrick mumbled, "I wish Vic would melt. Or molt."

"Look, I get it," Grace said. "Victor is loud and pushy and has some big-time boundary issues. But he's here, isn't he? He shows up."

"Whether you want him to or not." Patrick slipped into the waiter's coat.

"Well, I always heard showing up was ninety percent of the job. Lots of fathers don't even do that." She brushed off the back of Patrick's jacket.

"He's not my father," Patrick said.

"Well, that's too bad," Grace said, "because it pretty much leaves you without one." Grace went back to the living room, leaving Patrick alone.

Patrick considered her words, then with a final check in the mirror, followed her out.

Neither of them noticed that Victor had been sitting out on the balcony. He'd overheard the whole conversation. Feeling sad and rejected, his wings sagged.

"All right, guys. Game on," Patrick rallied the Smurfs.

"I'll stay here with Blue," Grace said.

"And Vic," Patrick quickly added.

"Actually . . . ," Victor began.

Patrick put up a hand. "No 'actuallys.' And this time I mean it!" To the Smurfs, Patrick said, "Let's go."

"We're gonna get Smurfette this time. One hundred percent guaranteed!" Grouchy headed to the door.

Everyone stopped. In one single movement, they all looked at Grouchy.

"What did you just say, Grouchy?" Papa cleaned his ears.

"Don't call me Grouchy anymore," Grouchy said. "I am changing my tune. From now on I am Positive Smurf." Ex-Grouchy put his hands on his hips and tossed back his head. "Ow, I hurt my back."

"You'll get the hang of it," Papa assured him.

Azrael entered the Hôtel Plaza Athénée, all wet and muddy.

"Ah, *le chat* VIP," a bellman said, eyeing the cat. "Please, I will take you to your room."

The bellman led Azrael to the elevator. As they

passed the front desk, a clerk answered the phone, saying, "Room service."

In a cab outside the hotel, Patrick was the one making the call. In his best Gargamel impersonation, Patrick said, "Listen well, you slack-jawed knave."

The ruse worked. "Hello, Monsieur Gargamel," the clerk said.

"I want ale, curds, and blistered meats sent to my room in ten minutes—or I will turn you into a legless tree sloth!" Patrick hung up and looked over at the Smurfs.

"How was that?" he asked, feeling satisfied he'd done well. They didn't answer. "Smurrrrrfs?"

Apparently, he'd done too well. He'd frightened Clumsy and Grouchy. They hid their faces behind Papa.

"Guys, relax. I'm just messing with you," Patrick said.

"That is just not funny, Master Winslow," Papa replied.

Grace and Blue were taking a nap. Victor was bored. He paced the hotel room, then sat for a while to look at pictures of birds.

"Duck. Duck. Duck. Goose." He flipped through the

photos.

Something on the floor caught his eye. A white plastic hotel card. Victor went to pick it up.

"Whoa! Patrick's key card. He's gonna need this." Victor looked at the open window. "I'll show him I'm more than just some eccentric waterfowl!"

Patrick entered the hotel kitchen, dressed like a waiter. He easily found the food cart marked: MSSR GARGAMEL. SUITE NAPOLÉON.

"Le bingo," Patrick said. Acting like he was on the job, Patrick pushed the cart past the double doors and into the service hallway. He opened his coat and the Smurfs slid out.

"Okay, guys, listen. When we get in the room, if there's any problem . . ." While he spoke, the Smurfs sat down on a plate and Patrick covered them with a large silver dome.

"There's no such thing as problems, my friend. Only smurfitunities," Grouchy said from their hiding place.

"You're freaking me out, Grouchy." Vanity shivered.

"I'm Positive Smurf!" Grouchy grumbled.

Patrick entered the elevator, slid the service key card through the slot, and hit the top button.

A whispered voice made him hold the door.

"Psst. Patrick Winslow-Doyle!"

Patrick stuck his head out the elevator to find Victor hiding behind a plant.

"What are you doing here?" Patrick whispered-yelled.

"Saving your tail feather," Victor said. "Now, c'mere! I got something you need for your mission."

Patrick stepped out of the elevator.

"Hurry up. There's no time to argue!" Victor showed him the white square he'd found. "It's the security card for the elevator."

Patrick held out the card he'd brought with him. "I have the security card." He pointed at Victor's hand. "That's our room key."

Victor lost a few feathers. "Oh." Then he said, "Well, now, when you come back, you'll be able to get in—no problem." He handed the key to Patrick. "You're welcome."

Patrick turned to go, but just then the elevator doors began to close. Patrick rushed forward quickly, but wasn't fast enough. The elevator was headed up without him.

"No!" Patrick shouted, banging on the door.

Victor could only sigh.

Patrick was so mad, he wouldn't look at his stepfather.

A sous-chef passed them standing by the elevator. The

man was wearing a large set of red headphones, head bobbing to the music. He found the duck hiding behind a plant.

"How did you get out?! We need you for the duck à l'orange!" The chef grabbed Victor.

"Put me down!"

The sous-chef couldn't hear Victor over the music in his headphones.

"Hey! You wanna piece of me?" Victor protested as they passed a sign that said: SPÉCIALE DE CE SOIR—DUCK À L'ORANGE. "No, no, no, that's not what I meant."

Victor looked back over his shoulder at Patrick, wide-eyed. "Oh sure, it starts with the ducks, but soon, no one is safe!"

"Unbelievable." Patrick shook his head.

The tray of food had gone up to Gargamel's penthouse with the Smurfs onboard. Victor was going into the kitchen to be cooked for dinner.

Patrick didn't know what to do.

At the last minute he decided the Smurfs would be okay. Victor needed him more.

Chapter 12

The service elevator opened, but no one pushed the cart out into the hall.

The domed lid tilted up and the Smurfs peeked out.

Papa looked around. "Master Winslow? Where are you?"

He dropped the lid back down as a room service waiter noticed the cart. The man checked the ticket and searched around for whoever was meant to be delivering it. Finding no one else, he delivered the cart to the penthouse.

Gargamel was downstairs in the hotel lobby.

He passed a doorman bending down to tie his shoe, and that made the wizard happy.

"Aargamel the Perfect be praised. Finally. Someone

gets me!" Gargamel noted the kneeling doorman to a passing tourist. "Is this so hard?"

The tourist didn't understand.

The room service waiter pushed the food cart inside, where Azrael was lounging on an ottoman.

"'Allo, kee-tee. 'Ere is your room service." The waiter prepared to serve the meal.

"We're in," Papa whispered to the Smurfs hiding under the domed lid.

"What do we do now?" Vanity asked.

Clumsy knew. "What Gutsy would do: kick blue butt and take names at a later time. Let's light this fuse!"

Before the others could slow him down, Clumsy threw off the lid and struck a karate pose. "Hiii-yaaa!" Clumsy looked tough for a moment, but then he slipped. "Ahhhhhhh!"

"Ahhhhhhh!" the waiter screamed back at him. The man shoved the cart away and rushed for the door.

The cart rolled toward the open French doors but was too wide to fit past them.

CLUNK!

It slammed to a stop in the doorway. Caught in the cascade of food and plates, the Smurfs slipped all the way across the balcony, barely holding on to the iron railing to keep from going over the side. Relieved, Grouchy glanced down at the five-story drop. They were lucky.

Grouchy turned to Clumsy. "Are you smurfin' kidding me?! You nearly—" He remembered his new positive outlook. "I mean, good try."

Vanity crawled out of the mess. "Oh. My. Smurf. I'm covered in filth."

With a loud hiss, Azrael suddenly jumped up onto the cart.

Vanity noticed himself reflected in the cat's eyes. "But I admit, I wear it well." Quick as he could, Vanity climbed back over the ledge and dove into the food wreckage with the other Smurfs close behind. Azrael leaped at them, but while in midair, two storks flew through the open French doors and knocked Azrael back into the penthouse living room.

The storks entered the suite, flapping madly. One bird knocked a champagne bucket over. It fell on Azrael, trapping him underneath.

"That will do, stork," Smurfette said.

Vexy and Smurfette shooed the storks out, and then Hackus slammed the balcony doors shut. The door latch fell into place. The suite was locked shut, with Papa and the others trapped outside.

"That was awesome!" Vexy cheered.

"High fours!" Smurfette high-foured Vexy, then held

her palm up for Hackus to smack.

"Hackus happy! Hackus happy!" He tagged her hand. "BWAMOOOAGAGAMOOGA!"

Smurfette turned to Vexy. Feeling emotional about having had the best day ever, she impulsively hugged Vexy.

"What are you doing?!" Vexy pulled back.

"I'm just hugging you," Smurfette said, letting go. "Haven't you ever been hugged?"

Vexy was silent for such a long time that Smurfette knew the answer. She stepped up and hugged Vexy again.

"Hackus hug! Hackus hug!" Hackus threw his arms around the two of them for a group hug.

The Smurfs pressed their noses to the hotel suite's doors.

"There she is!" Clumsy pointed at Smurfette. "But she's hugging the pale Smurfs."

"What is she doing?" Grouchy wondered.

Smurfette moved away from her new friends and noticed her reflection in the balcony doors. The way the light shone through, she couldn't see the Smurfs outside. Her clothes were torn and dirty. Her hair chopped off on one side. She turned back to Vexy and Hackus. She fit in perfectly with them now.

"See?" Vexy stepped beside her. "Now that's the real you."

Smurfette nodded. Maybe this *was* the real her. . . .

Papa and the others began shouting for her attention.

"Smurfette! Smurfette!"

She didn't hear them.

"Wow, she's really let herself go," Vanity remarked.

"She's confused," Papa said, worried. "Help me get these doors open."

"It's called Smurfholm syndrome," Grouchy said as he tugged on the locked handle. "You become sympathetic to your captors."

"We have to get to her before she turns!" Papa pulled back to the edge of the balcony.

He and the Smurfs hit the glass doors at a full run. But the doors didn't open. The Smurfs bounced back, just as Gargamel entered the suite.

"Kindness . . . kindness . . . kindness . . ." He repeated the word, as if saying it over and over would make the idea stick. "Ahem. Little children, Daddy's home! And he brought presents—in order to express kindness toward you!"

The Smurfs were about to start another rush for the

doors but froze instead.

"Gargamel!" Papa said breathlessly.

"He's gonna kill her!" Clumsy panicked. "We have to get her out of there!"

They tried and tried to open the doors, but they wouldn't budge.

Gargamel handed Smurfette a wrapped present.

"I think we got off on the wrong foot. Happy birthday, my dear. Seems like only yesterday you were my little gob of clay and assorted putrid ingredients."

Smurfette was surprised. "You remembered my birthday?"

"Of course." Gargamel gave her his best smile. "We're family. Families don't forget things like that." He added, "By the way, your little blue step-papa never came, did he? I'm so sorry. That must really sting. Perhaps this little trinket will cheer you up." Smurfette looked at the gift. Gargamel said, "Happy birthday."

Papa and the others watched as Smurfette accepted the gift from Gargamel.

"Oh no." Papa shook his head sadly.

In the hotel kitchen, Patrick was searching for Victor. He snuck into a storage area where there was a caged-off section. A dozen live ducks wandered around. Patrick sneezed, then said, "All right, if it looks like a duck, quacks like a duck, and smells like a corn dog . . ."

One duck raised its wing. "Hey, those corn dogs put a roof over your head!"

"Let's go." Patrick reached out for Victor, but Victor moved back.

"Whoa, whoa, whoa! What about my brothers? We can't just leave them here to get eaten." Victor shook his tail feathers.

"You just met them!" Patrick did not have time for this!

Victor put his wings around two ducks. "This is my flock," he said. "I can't just leave 'em behind."

Patrick couldn't believe it. He almost wished he'd gone after the Smurfs instead.

Up in the hotel suite, Smurfette was holding her present.

"Go ahead, my dear. Open your gift," Gargamel said.

When Smurfette didn't start right away, Hackus decided to help. He grabbed the gift and began tearing the paper.

"Hackus open! Hackus open!"

It was the Gargamel action figure and wand.

Hackus imitated the wizard. "Bow! Kneel! BWAMO-OOAGAGAMOOGA!"

Smurfette and Vexy laughed.

"Ha, ha, ha. Delightful rendition," Gargamel said. Then he softly muttered, "Keep it up, No Neck, and I'll turn you into a cross-eyed newt."

Hackus zipped his lips.

Smurfette picked up the tiny wand and examined it.

"Yes. A wand of your very own. Do you like it?" He squinted at the useless plastic. "Oh, silly me. I forgot to turn it on." Gargamel poured one drop of essence into her wand. "There we are. Go on. Don't be afraid."

Smurfette considered the power, then turned the wand toward Gargamel. "How do you know I won't use it on you?"

Gargamel clearly hadn't thought of that possibility. "How do I—I—" The right words came to him. "Because, Smurfette, I am your father. Search your feelings—you know it to be true."

Smurfette looked at the wand, then looked at Gargamel. Then at the wand again.

Outside, Grouchy shouted, "She's gonna zap him!"

"Get him, Smurfette!" Clumsy said.

But Smurfette didn't zap Gargamel. First, she fired at the wet bar. Bottles popped. Champagne flooded everywhere in arching fountains.

The Naughties cheered.

"Can you sing the La La song?" Smurfette asked Gargamel.

"I'd rather not," Gargamel replied.

"Please," Smurfette begged. "It's what I do at home."

With a groan, Gargamel reluctantly began to sing the song.

Smurfette suddenly turned and zapped the upside-down champagne bucket. It flew against the wall. Azrael tumbled out a moment before the bucket fell and conked him on his head.

The Naughties laughed some more.

Gargamel stepped up behind Smurfette, holding his wand—just like in her nightmare.

"Wonderful. Wonderful," he chuckled.

The Smurfs couldn't believe what they were witnessing.

"Papa, what's happening?" Clumsy asked as Smurfette took aim at the giant mirror on the wall.

In the mirror, it looked like she was pointing the

wand at them, even though it was at her reflection.

"No!" Papa warned. But it was too late. The bolt of magical energy rebounded off the mirror, straight through the glass balcony doors. The doors crashed open, and the blue flame blasted the Smurfs over the side of the balcony—to their doom.

Chapter 13

Patrick freed the ducks, and they all ran out the back door of the hotel.

Victor yelled, "Take to the skies, lads! Free at last! Free at last!"

"What are you? Martin Luther Wing?" Patrick asked sarcastically.

"Don't lecture me, Mr. Patrick I-don't-ever-make-any-mistakes-hyphen-Doyle." Victor was interrupted by four sharp screams.

"What the *QUACK* is that?!" Victor looked up to find Papa, Clumsy, Vanity, and Grouchy hurling through the air toward the hard cement.

Victor extended his wing. *WOOMF!* The wing turned to a hand.

"Uh-oh," Victor said.

Still ready to help, Victor glided under the Smurfs,

but then his ducky body began to twitch.

POOF!

Victor became human again.

One problem: He was completely naked.

The Smurfs crash-landed onto Victor's back, forcing them all at high speed into a huge laundry bin full of dirty sheets and towels.

"What happened?" Victor said from beneath the Smurfs.

Papa, Clumsy, and Grouchy popped up.

"Hellooo!"

Victor looked around for the source of the voice.

He reached into the laundry and pulled out Vanity.

"Oh, the shame." Vanity quickly adjusted his hat.

Just as they were getting out of the bin, a team of security guards chased them all away.

Smurfette was exploring the power of her wand with the Naughties. Across the suite, Azrael crept up to Gargamel and said, "Meow."

"What do you mean the Smurfs were here? In this room? Why didn't you say so?"

Azrael moaned.

Gargamel glanced at Smurfette. "She mustn't learn of this. We have to get her away from here—and obtain the formula—NOW!" In a sweet voice he called out, "Smurfette, are you ready to go celebrate, my dear?"

Patrick and Victor went back to the hotel. Grace and Blue were waiting for news.

"We were this close to getting Smurfette back. Now, who knows what Gargamel's doing with her? All thanks to that walking corn dog disaster." Patrick glared at his stepfather.

"Okay, indoor voice. And remember to breathe," Grace said.

"I want him gone!" Patrick was mad.

"Patrick, he's your dad," Grace reminded him.

"Nope. That's one thing he's not!" Patrick shook his head.

"He's right, Grace." Victor entered the living room, dressed. "I'm not his father. His real father left and started a new family. And he's been mad about it ever since."

Patrick held up a hand. "Okay, you know what? You can just stop right there."

"And so he should be," Victor went on. "But I can't take the brunt of it, anymore."

"Hey, I never asked you to come barging into my life, okay?" Patrick said. "I didn't ask you to marry my mother. Or take away Zeus."

"Zeus? The pigeon?" Victor wrinkled his forehead.

"The parrot. My parrot. Taken away because you were allergic," Patrick told him.

"Whoa! I was not allergic to that bird," Victor said.

"Yes, you were!" Patrick said.

"No, I wasn't!" Victor paused. "You were."

"What?" Patrick had no idea what he meant.

"Yeah. That's right," Victor explained. "It got so bad. Every day you were wheezing. But your mother and I knew it would break your heart to think the bird had to go away because of you. You already blamed yourself for your father. So I took the heat."

Patrick paced the room. "That's a lie. I am not allergic to birds."

"Oh, really?" Victor handed him some of the leftover duck feathers. "Go ahead, big man. Sniff my feathers. Go ahead. Sniff!"

Patrick took the feathers from Victor and sniffed a big sniff to prove he wasn't allergic.

"ACHOOOO!" Patrick sneezed.

"Yeah! The truth itches, doesn't it?"

Patrick didn't know what to say.

"Listen to me, Patrick. I loved your mother with all my heart. I took care of Jeannette, and I made her happy. And I chose to love you as my own. I didn't have to do that. But you were a kid with no father—no hope in your eyes, a big hole in your heart. So I gave you everything I could. But now . . . I'm done. You made that pretty clear. So here's my last words of advice: grow up. Be a man. Stop blaming everyone else for your pain." He pointed at Blue. "And whatever you do, don't teach that beautiful son of yours that love is conditional. 'Cause it's not."

Victor stepped over and kissed Blue on the head.

"Grampa Vicster."

With a small smile to Grace, Victor headed for the door. "Good-bye, Patrick Winslow." He walked out.

Grace and Blue looked at Patrick.

"You're just gonna let him leave?" Grace asked.

Patrick didn't answer. He stared at the floor.

"Wow," Grace said. She took Blue into the bedroom.

"Blue . . . ," Patrick whispered his son's name as the door shut between them.

Smurfette's birthday party began with a ride on the grand Ferris wheel of Paris. Around the large wheel were booths and games. A band was playing. The streets were crowded with tourists from various nations. Gargamel, Smurfette, and the Naughties stood in the Ferris wheel line together, taking it all in.

"There're a lot of people," Smurfette exclaimed.

"I prefer to call them admirers." Gargamel raised his

wand. *"ALAKNEEL!"* With a blue light zap, the people in line all fell to their knees, creating a broad path to the wheel.

A mime actor pretending to be trapped inside a box didn't kneel, so Gargamel blasted him into an actual glass box. The mime screamed and pounded on the glass.

Ignoring him, Gargamel turned to Smurfette. "Shall we?" He led the way to the front of the line.

As they passed, several people recognized Gargamel. They were excited to see a celebrity. "There's Gargamel," a man said.

"Hello, yes, it's me," Gargamel said.

"C'est magnifique!" a woman cooed.

"Hello, nice to see you. Don't look me in the eye, please." Gargamel swept his cloak around himself.

"Look at those magical creatures, Mom!" A little boy pointed.

"These are my children. Please don't touch the Naughties." He proudly said, "It's my daughter's birthday. Coming through. Come, children, don't dawdle." Then to the operator running the ride, Gargamel asked, "What are you looking at? I have a—how do you say—fast pass."

At the wheel's entrance, Gargamel used magic to toss out a Swedish couple. "Thank you for keeping our seat warm. *ALAKAZOUT!*" Gargamel, Smurfette, and the Naughties climbed in.

"Father, it's feeding time soon," Vexy said.

"Not now!" Gargamel told her.

"But, Father." She tried again to get his attention.

"I said not now!" Turning to Smurfette, Gargamel said, "Our fun is just beginning. *ALAKAZELEVATE!*" The Ferris wheel began to turn, carrying them to the very top. "Why do they call it the Ferret's wheel. I see no ferrets," Gargamel remarked as he looked out at the skyline. "Ahhhh. Isn't this lovely? Just think, Smurfette. With your essence and my magic, there is absolutely nothing we cannot do."

"Then why are we going so slow?" With a mischievous look in her eye, Smurfette flicked her wand. The giant wheel began to spin faster and faster until—*CLANG!*

The wheel broke free and rolled through the street.

"Whoa. You really have a flair for this," Gargamel noted as people on the wheel screamed. On the ground, families fled in panic from the sidewalk cafés and restaurants.

A Chinese visitor asked his children, "Louvre, schmoovre! Who wants to ride the wheel?"

The kids all raised their hands as the wheel rolled by.

At Patrick and Grace's hotel room, Papa stood on the balcony, looking out at the lights of the city.

Patrick stepped outside. "Oh, sorry. I was just looking for a place to think."

"Please join me. I was doing a little thinking myself." Papa made room for Patrick next to him.

"Master Winslow, can I ask you some advice? Papa to papa," Papa Smurf asked.

"You want papa advice from me?" Patrick asked.

"Why wouldn't I? I've seen the bond you've forged with young Blue." Papa tipped his head toward the bedroom.

"I got some good advice once," Patrick said with a small smile.

"And now I could use some," Papa told him. "It's about Smurfette. A little secret I've kept to myself, something she doesn't know. See, when I turned her into a Smurf, well, it wasn't a complete transformation." Papa's eyes grew dark as he remembered. "I worked my strongest magic, but she's still Gargamel's creation." With a shiver, Papa continued, "She's a Smurf only so long as she chooses to be. She isn't aware of that. But if she chooses otherwise, well . . ." He paused and looked up at Patrick. "Do you think I've done enough?"

"Are you kidding? Gargamel just made her, but you . . . You made her what she is. You stepped in and loved her as your very own. No one asked you to, but you did. Because you knew she needed you." Patrick realized what he was saying also applied to what Victor had done for him as a boy. "That's a pretty special kind of love. She's way too smart not to see that."

Papa said, "I hope you're right. I don't care where she came from. I love her just the same."

Patrick sat silently for a long moment.

"Thank you, Master Winslow." Papa headed back inside. "That was exactly what I needed to hear."

"Me too," Patrick mumbled to himself.

Clumsy and Grouchy were washing up at the bathroom sink, getting ready for bed, when Papa burst in, full of new energy.

"Let's go, Smurfs," he said.

"Where?" Grouchy asked.

"We're getting Smurfette. We know what Gargamel wants and where he'll be taking her." Papa wanted them to move faster.

"But you saw her. She's one of them now," Clumsy said.

"You listen to me, Clumsy Smurf. We rise to the amount of love we're shown, and we sink only when that love stops. We didn't believe in Smurfette because she changed; she changed because we believed in her." He pointed to the door. "And we're not about to stop now."

"Yeah. Stop being so negative." Grouchy tapped Clumsy on the head.

Clumsy nodded. "My bad."

Patrick stuck his head into the bathroom. He was wearing a big coat.

"Master Winslow! You're coming with us?" Papa asked.

"Is a Smurf's butt blue?" Patrick replied with a wink.

Grouchy bent over and took a look at his own rear end. "You tell me."

Papa laughed. "C'mon. Let's get smurfing!"

The Smurfs started toward the opera house. Through the mist, they marched with purpose. Patrick was armed with a fire poker. The Smurfs had mini-flashlights.

The sewer grate they'd escaped from earlier was blocked.

"Oh dear," Vanity said.

"This is how we came out before." Papa looked around for another way in.

"Now what?" Grouchy asked.

"Over here, guys!" Clumsy found a Smurf-size storm drain nearby.

Vanity looked at the drain, then at Patrick. "But what about Master Winslow?"

"You guys go on," Patrick told them. "I saw a manhole cover back there. I'll make my way in, you guys find Smurfette, and I'll meet up with you."

"You're a good man, Master Winslow," Papa said as he slipped into the storm drain.

"Yeah, well, you're a good Smurf. See you soon," Patrick promised, and jogged away.

Chapter 14

Gargamel led Smurfette and the Naughties into his lab. The giant, evil Smurfalator was shrouded in darkness. Azrael was already there, waiting.

"Why are we coming down here, Father?" Vexy asked.

"We are celebrating your long-lost sister's birthday. We can't very well end the revelry without a cake." Gargamel waved his wand. A birthday cake floated across the room and landed in front of Smurfette. With another wave of the dragon wand, candles burned brightly.

"It's your favorite, Smurfette. Blue velvet. Now, make a wish. Anything your tiny little heart can dream of, it is yours," Gargamel said.

"Anything?" Smurfette asked.

"But of course," Gargamel told her.

"Meow," Azrael warned.

"Well, within reason. We are on somewhat of an essence budget. That's why I need the formula," Gargamel said.

Smurfette didn't blow the candles out right away. She looked at the flickering lights, uncertain what she wanted. She was happy, but was it a good kind of happy?

While Smurfette tried to sort out her feelings, the Smurfs rappelled down from the ceiling of the lair. They stopped on a ledge, high above the lab.

"There she is," Vanity whispered.

Papa gave directions. "Vanity, you come with me. Clumsy and Grouchy, find Master Winslow."

"C'mon, partner," Clumsy told Grouchy. "We move swiftly like the wind. We become one with the night and arrive before anyone knows we have left. Let's go!" Clumsy turned to run but face-planted instead.

"Sometimes the wind is loud." Grouchy shook his head.

Patrick was still trying to pry open the manhole cover, using the iron fire poker, when Victor showed up.

"Victor? What are you doing here?" Patrick asked, surprised.

"Grace told me where you'd be. She said you might need a hand," Victor told him.

Patrick struggled to move the manhole cover. "Did she?"

Feeling rejected again, Victor lowered his shoulders as he turned to leave.

"Victor, wait," Patrick called out. "As usual, Grace is right. I could use some help."

"Well, for starters, you might try lifting the sewer cover." He indicated a different place on the street. "'Unless you're planning on fixing the phone lines."

Sure enough, upon closer look, Patrick had been breaking into the city's phone lines. He laughed at his mistake.

Victor reached out his hand. Patrick shook it.

"Actually"—Victor raised his eyebrows—"I meant gimme the poker. But, thanks, I appreciate the handshake."

With another small chuckle, Patrick handed Victor the fire poker, and an instant later, the two of them lifted the correct sewer cover together.

Smurfette hadn't made her wish or blown out her candles. Gargamel was growing impatient.

"Smurfette," he said. "The formula. Take all the time

you need. As long as it's very soon."

"Then we can all be blue. Together," Vexy said.

"Hackus blue! Hackus blue!" Hackus chanted.

"Awww. They want to be blue—just like their big sister," Gargamel said in a sweet voice.

"Then we could be a real family." Vexy's eyes were wet with tears.

"This is a sacred gift entrusted to me," Smurfette said at last. She backed away from the cake. "I'm sorry. I just can't."

Gargamel exploded in anger. "What do you mean you can't?! I've given you everything! Kindness! Presents! A cake with no poison!" He began to shout. "IT'S BEEN HORRIBLE! Now you will give me what I want—RIGHT NOW! The formula!"

Smurfette put her hands on her hips. "No!"

Gargamel was furious. His face turned red and his hands shook.

Vexy called in a weak voice, "Um . . . Father . . ."

Gargamel and Smurfette faced the Naughties. They didn't look good.

"Hackus dizzy." *WHAM!* Hackus fell over.

"What's happening to them?!" Smurfette was worried.

"Don't tell me you actually *care* for these creatures. How pathetic for you." Gargamel grimaced, but then his tone changed. "And how perfect for me!"

Clumsy and Grouchy hurried through the sewer tunnels until they spotted Patrick and Victor. "Master Winslow! We found her," Clumsy said, talking at full speed.

"Gargamel's got her," Grouchy said.

"In the room with that awful machine!" Clumsy was very upset.

Patrick kept calm. "Let's go."

They began to run, but quickly noticed that Victor wasn't with them. Patrick went back. "What are you doing?"

"I've got machines all over my plant. But when the power goes out, we've got no corn dogs." Victor was studying the overhead wiring.

"Victor, we really don't have time for corn d—" Patrick began when Victor pointed at a sign.

It read GÉNÉRATEUR ÉLECTRIQUE. And there was a high-voltage symbol under the words.

Papa and Vanity went on ahead until they reached a large pipe. Papa marked the pathway with a piece of blue chalk. He drew an *S* outside the pipe, then said, "This way!" The two Smurfs climbed inside.

Smurfette watched in horror as the Naughties faded to white, their hair turned gray, and their skin wrinkled.

"I'm so sorry. I thought you knew," Gargamel said with a wicked frown. "Without essence, they cannot live."

Hackus fell to his knees.

"Father, please." Vexy begged for her life.

"Give them what you have! Take some from me!" Smurfette held out a lock of her hair.

"Why? What's the point? You won't give me the formula, so I might as well just let them go." Gargamel turned away.

"You mean let them die?!" Smurfette exclaimed.

Gargamel shrugged. "I can always make others. Besides, I'm not the one letting them die."

Vexy looked to Smurfette with desperate eyes.

"Okay, okay! I'll give it to you!" Smurfette gave up. "Feed them!"

"Eh, eh, eh! The formula first." Gargamel held back his wand.

"Feed them!" Smurfette couldn't wait another minute.

"The formula." Gargamel slid a piece of paper toward her and held out a pen.

And Smurfette began to write.

Papa and Vanity reached the end of the sewer pipe. It was a dead end. They could hear voices on the other side.

Papa called out, but only his echo called back.

"Wait, I know!" Vanity exclaimed. He extended his arm through the metal grate and held out his mirror. In the reflection, Papa could see around the corner into Gargamel's lair.

Smurfette was finishing the formula's recipe. "Four hopeful thoughts, a dab of royal jelly, mimosa pollen, and a drop of mink oil. And you must say one loving truth. There. That's the formula Papa used." She handed Gargamel the page.

"Oh, Smurfette." Papa put his head against the side of the pipe and sighed sadly.

"Now feed them!" Smurfette told Gargamel.

Papa raised his head. He suddenly understood what was happening.

"First, we are going to see if it works." Gargamel snapped his fingers. Lights came on in a brewing area. A caldron bubbled. The doors of a large cabinet swung open. Magic ingredients were on every shelf.

Victor busted the electrical panel door. He, Patrick, Clumsy, and Grouchy were thrilled until they discovered the generator was in a cage. The surrounding fence was broken.

"We got this!" Clumsy pointed to himself and Grouchy.

Clumsy and Grouchy headed for rusted holes in the metal fencing. Grouchy got through, but Clumsy tripped on a broken wire. Grouchy turned back to give him a helping hand.

"Thanks, Grouchy," Clumsy said.

"You know, in the past, I would have laughed when you fell. But it's the new me. I realized I can still laugh at you and help out at the same time." Grouchy grinned.

It didn't take long for Gargamel to finish the brew. But by the time he had the potion ready, the Naughties were on the floor, near death.

"Hurry!" Smurfette urged Gargamel.

From the wizard's cauldron rose long fingers of brilliant, blue, shining liquid.

Spouts of potion rose through the air and went directly into the Naughties' mouths. Almost immediately, the Naughties felt better, and an instant later, they began to turn blue.

"Oh. My. Smurrrrrf! It worked! It worked! The world is mine! I can make my own Smurfs!" Weeping with joy, Gargamel dropped to one knee. The second the Naughties became fully healthy, Gargamel snatched them up. "Into the machine! The machine!"

Gargamel held Hackus in his hand. "Oh, finally. You're a real boy." Then he dumped him into the Smurfalator. "Now, off you go. Into the machine. All of you! Bye-bye! Au revoir! *Adeus! Zai jian!*"

From behind the pipe's grate, Papa watched Gargamel struggling to shove Smurfette into the machine. Papa kicked frantically at the grate, but it wouldn't budge. Just then Vanity rotated his mirror slightly to reveal a pin sticking out of the grate's hinge.

"Papa, wait!" Papa stopped kicking as Vanity stretched his arm forward. The pin was just out of reach.

Gargamel strapped Vexy into the machine, next to Smurfette and Hackus.

"You . . . face . . . leaking." Hackus noticed Smurfette's tears. His own eyes begin to water.

"Hackus leaking! Hackus leaking!"

Vexy turned her head to face Smurfette. "You sacrificed everything—just to save us."

"I had to," Smurfette said. "I care about you."

"WAHH!" Hackus started to bawl hysterically.

"Yes, yes. Let it all out. Smurfy tears are just chock-full of essence." And Gargamel began to collect Hackus's tears in a jar.

Vanity reached for the grate's pin. His face was pressed against the dirty bars, but it didn't even matter to him. All that mattered was helping Smurfette.

Clumsy and Grouchy were standing on a metal ledge halfway up the front of the generator. Patrick and Victor were behind a fence.

"Try throwing that lever!" Patrick pointed up. In order to reach it, one Smurf was going to have to get on the other's shoulders.

"You go. I got you," Clumsy told Grouchy.

"You got me? You barely got you," Grouchy said, but still he climbed up. Standing on Clumsy, Grouchy was the perfect height. He wiped away the grease on both sides of the lever, revealing a positive sign and a negative sign.

"Which way?" Grouchy called out to Patrick.

Patrick didn't know. Victor didn't either.

"Try negative," Patrick suggested. "It might shut it off."

Grouchy thought for a moment, then said, "No. You gotta be positive." He pulled the lever to the positive sign.

ZZZZZZ! Grouchy was zapped with an electric bolt.

BAAAM! He was blasted backward, smashing into a wall and falling into a bucket.

FOOMP! The lights went out.

Chapter 15

"Grouchy, you did it!" Patrick cheered.

"Yes! We are heroes!" Victor and Clumsy shouted at the same time.

Grouchy stuck his head up from out the bucket. His blue skin was covered with black soot. "Why did I doubt negative?" He groaned.

While the Smurfs were turning off the generator, Gargamel reached for the switch of his great machine. "One small step for wizards, one giant leap for *ME*!"

"Meow!"

"Yes, yes, you can push the button," Gargamel told the cat.

He lifted Azrael, and the cat put out his paw.

"One giant leap for—" Gargamel began again.

FOOMP!

When Azrael flipped the switch, the power went out. The lab went completely dark.

Gargamel finished his thought. "For cats who apparently can't even push a button properly."

FOOMP! It went dark in the pipe.

FOOMP! FOOMP! The lights of Paris suddenly went out.

"Son of a smurf!" Gargamel cursed. The only light in his lair was from the moonlight drifting in from a ceiling grate. "Come, Azrael," Gargamel said. "It appears we must harness the power of the skies one last time." He headed for the exit, muttering, "I am but a simple wizard on the cusp of world domination. Why does it have to be so . . . so . . . *Les Misérables*?"

"Got it!" Vanity finally reached the grate's pin.

"Good work, Vanity!" Papa said, filled with hope.

The grate opened. Vanity and Papa rushed into the lair.

"Smurfette!" Papa hurried to her side.

"Papa?! Is that you? You came for me?" Smurfette asked, her voice weak.

"Of course we came for you! Was there ever a question?" Papa worked to set Smurfette free.

On the rooftop of the opera house, Gargamel jammed a huge electrical cable into a statue of Apollo, between the strings of the god's harp.

"Here. Hold this," Gargamel told the statue.

Using his wand, Gargamel whipped up another magical storm.

KKKRACKKK!

Lightning rippled through the sky and hit the cable. The statue glowed.

"Papa, I gave Gargamel the formula!" Smurfette admitted.

"She saved our lives," Vexy explained. She and Hackus were still strapped to the machine.

"Hackus live! Hackus live!"

"I am so sorry," Smurfette told Papa Smurf.

Patrick, Victor, Grouchy, and Clumsy rushed through the sewer.

Clumsy found the blue *S*. "Papa left a mark!"

The pipe was Smurf-size. "Go. We'll find a door,"

Patrick said to Clumsy and Grouchy.

Clumsy and Grouchy crawled into the pipe.

"Smurfette." Papa helped her out of the Smurfalator and brought her close. "A life is the most precious thing to protect. I'm proud of you." He hugged her tight.

"You . . . you are?" She wasn't expecting him to say he was proud.

"Seriously? No spanking? No smack to the knuckles? You forgive her, just like that?" Vexy asked.

"Of course. I love her," Papa Smurf said.

Because of all the emotion, Hackus began crying wildly. "Leaking again."

Just then Grouchy and Clumsy leaped out of the sewer pipe. Clumsy tripped, then converted it into a somersault and a karate pose. "I meant to do that," he said, looking around the lair to see who saw him. "Oh, who am I kidding?"

"You found Smurfette!" Grouchy said to Papa and Vanity.

FOOOOOM!

All of a sudden the power came back on.

"Finally some decent lighting," Vanity said.

"Let's get the smurf out of here!" Clumsy suggested.

"Wait!" Smurfette waved a hand toward Vexy and Hackus. "What about them?"

"What about 'em?" Grouchy asked. "They kidnapped you."

"They're Gargamel's," Clumsy reminded her.

Smurfette glanced at Papa. "So was I, but Papa—he never gave up on me. And I'm not about to give up on them."

Papa stepped forward and put an arm across Smurfette's shoulder. "And you thought you weren't a Smurf." He smiled at her. Then to the others, he said, "Unstrap them. Quickly!"

"And then there were six." Gargamel's voice boomed through the lair.

In the excitement, the Smurfs had let down their guard. They hadn't noticed Gargamel had returned.

The wizard raised his wand. "Well, six and a half if you count Hackus." Blue energy began to swirl, filling the room with an evil mist.

Gargamel quickly trapped all the Smurfs. They were strapped into the Smurfalator, and the vat was filling quickly with smoky-blue wisps of energy.

Grouchy, still blackened from his earlier electrocution,

was shaking as the machine pumped and squeezed him.

"This . . . should . . . be . . . Hef . . . ty!" He wheezed.

Gargamel bubbled with joy.

"You said this wasn't going to hurt!" Vexy moaned in pain.

"Me. It's not going to hurt me," Gargamel clarified. "For you, it's going to be excruciating."

Papa struggled against the straps. "That's enough, Gargamel." He tipped his head toward the collection area. "You have enough."

"Yes, but you see I want more than enough!" Gargamel turned up the power.

The Smurfs moaned as they were squeezed even harder.

"Does anyone have a mint?" Vanity asked. "If it's going to be my last breath, I want it to be fresh."

Gargamel showed them a huge wand in the shape of a large, evil dragon. "I must be able to power this!" His small dragon wand was puny by comparison. "I call her Le Wanda! She sounds nice, but she's nooooott." The wizard placed Le Wanda under the essence tap, letting it fill up. He hulked. "Oh my. Whatever will I do with all this power? Oh, that's right. *I'M GOING TO RULE THE ENTIRE WORLD!*"

Gargamel turned to Papa Smurf. "Oh, and Papa, my first official act will be to create a portal directly from

Smurf Village to my Smurfalator, so all your little Smurfs can be here with you. Forever."

"I don't think so, Gargamel." Patrick stormed into the lair. Victor was right behind him. They stepped onto the top of the glass vat.

"You messed with the wrong Smurfs!" Victor announced.

"We're not Smurfs. They're the Smurfs," Patrick whispered.

"Today, we are all Smurfs!" Victor tightened his fists.

Gargamel raised his wand as Patrick swung at the essence vat with his iron poker. The glass didn't break.

"Put some back into it!" Victor took the poker and tried hitting it himself.

Patrick tried to take back the poker, but Victor wouldn't let go. Victor said, "Give it to me" at the same time Patrick said, "Not like that, like this!"

"Oh, for the love of Smurf, work together!" Papa moaned.

Patrick and Victor looked at each other, then nodded. Together, they held the poker and rammed it into the glass. The vat shattered. Wisps of Smurf essence flooded the room. The Naughties, the Smurfs, Patrick, and Victor were caught up in the blue flow and carried into the sewer pipes.

Gargamel and Azrael were slammed against a

wall. The Smurf formula burned up in a hot blue flame.

Gargamel's under-earth lair transformed into a floral-covered garden.

KABOOM!

The wave of blue energy exploded through the sewer grates, filling the streets with beautiful, shimmering blue light. Flowerpots sprouted new blooms, buildings glowed with light, windows sparkled, the area around the opera house shimmered in the dark Paris night.

Smurfette was lying on the sidewalk. She sat up, rubbing her eyes.

Slowly, all the Smurfs sat up. They'd turned back to a healthy blue.

"Is everyone all right?" Patrick asked them.

Papa counted heads. "All smurfy and accounted for."

Patrick smiled, relieved.

A taxi pulled up near them, and Grace got out with Blue. "Patrick!" she called out.

Patrick ran to greet them. "Grace! Blue!" He hugged his family. "We did it!"

Smurfette looked around and discovered Vexy was still lying facedown on the grass. "Vexy!" She helped her up.

Both of them looked down to see their reflections in

a puddle. Vexy's skin was bright and smurfy blue.

"You did this for me?" Vexy asked, very happy.

"What are sisters for?"

The girls shared a heartfelt look.

"Smurfette!" Grace came to them.

"Oh, Grace!" Smurfette gave her a smurfing hug, then said, "Grace, this is Vexy. My *other* sister."

Grace smiled. "Well, that makes you my sister too."

Vexy held her hand over her heart.

"Are you okay?" Smurfette asked.

"Is this what happy feels like?" There were tears in Vexy's eyes.

Patrick, Blue, and Victor joined them. Hackus walked into the center of the group.

"Oh, and this is Hackus . . . my brother," Vexy said.

"Hackus! Hackus! Hackus!" Hackus called.

"Hackus, this is Grace and Patrick and"—Smurfette noticed the child standing nearby—"your baby!"

"Smurfette, this is Blue," Grace said.

"You did good, Grace. He's bluuuuetiful," Smurfette said.

"Who this? Who this?" Hackus pointed at Victor.

"Oh. That's Victor. He's . . ." Grace paused. She looked at Patrick.

Patrick looked at Victor and answered, "He's my dad." He added, "And Blue's pretty fantastic grandfather."

Victor grabbed Patrick and pulled him into a massive bear hug.

"Daddy and Vicster!" Blue cheered.

"I'm proud of you, Patrick Winslow," Grace said, grinning.

"Hyphen . . . Doyle," Patrick added.

"Hyphen Smurf," Papa put in.

Patrick glanced at him.

"You're family," Papa said.

With a big smile, Patrick pulled Papa into Victor's hug.

"We did it, guys. Smurf pound!" Clumsy held out his fists for a bump. "Vanity . . . Positive . . ."

"I ain't pounding nothing. I'm Grouchy Smurf again. And I got a lot of pent-up anger to vent!" Grouchy told Clumsy.

"I'm with you, Grouchy. We just gotta be who we are," Vanity agreed.

"Yeah. Besides, we love you no matter what." Clumsy lowered his fists.

"Hey, smurf it out your ears, both of you!" Grouchy smiled. "Whoo, that feels good! I'm back, baby."

From behind them an evil voice roared. "AND SO AM I!"

Chapter 16

Gargamel crawled out from the sewer, filthy and crazed with anger. He raised his enormous dragon wand at the terrified gang.

"Smmmmmmuuurrrfs! For those of you who missed it the first time, this is Le Wanda, which is a hilarious play on words!" Gargamel chuckled madly.

Vexy noticed a piece of metal near her feet. It was bent from the explosion. She and Smurfette locked eyes.

"All for one!" Vexy said.

"And naughty for all!" Smurfette finished.

Vexy stepped on one end. Smurfette jumped hard onto the other end. Vexy went flying toward Gargamel. At the last second, Vexy grabbed on to Gargamel's wand. He couldn't fire at them.

"What are you doing, you little ingrate? I am your father." Gargamel tried to shake her off.

"How could you be my father? I'm a Smurf!" Vexy told him proudly.

She pushed the wand down and bit the dragon on the butt! The wand roared, and energy exploded out from its mouth. Vexy dove off as Gargamel was blown into the sky. The force tossed Gargamel around. The blast whipped him down the street, crashing from building to building. Finally, Gargamel was flung through a sewer grate.

Below the city were ancient catacombs, filled with skulls and bones. Gargamel screamed like a baby as he crashed through a wall, which broke away. Gargamel was in a train station. The train came fast and knocked him into a stairwell, where the wand's blue energy blasted him up, high into the air, over the famous church at Notre Dame. He bounced between the historic tower bells.

BING! BONG! BING!

"Sanctuary!" Gargamel shouted before he was blasted, into the sky and finally landed on top of the Eiffel Tower. A crate at his feet had a label on it: BASTILLE DAY. Below the words was the symbol of an exploding firecracker.

"Why does it always have to be so—"

WHA-BOOM!

The top of the Eiffel Tower erupted into a huge explosion of fireworks.

A Chinese tourist on the street looked up. "Papa, is

that a man up there?" the boy asked his dad.

The father grabbed his son's hand. "It's time to get out of this country. It's too dangerous."

As the last of the fireworks erupted, Gargamel blasted up, up, up into the stratosphere.

The blue essence faded from the Paris streets, and everything was quiet. Things went back to normal, and it was time for the Smurfs to go home.

Papa held out the magic that would take them to Smurf Village. "We've only got five crystals."

"And now there're seven of us," Clumsy said.

"Well, I say, no Smurf left behind!" Smurfette took Hackus and Vexy by the hand. She considered the problem for a moment, then spotted her own miniature dragon wand laying in the street. Smurfette picked it up. "I think I got a shot or two left."

ZAP!

Smurfette turned the five crystals into seven.

"Wow, Smurfette! You're pretty good with that wand." Grace was impressed.

"It's kinda in my blood. Which used to plague me, but as someone wonderful once told me, it doesn't matter where you came from. What matters is who you choose to be." With that, Smurfette put an arm around

Papa. He smiled at her, full of love.

Patrick put his arm around Victor. Blue joined the circle of Winslow-Doyle men.

"We're going to miss you, Smurfs," Victor said.

"You could always name a corn dog after 'em," Patrick said with a wink.

"Now you're talking. We could use blue corn," Victor agreed.

"Smurf dogs! Yum!" Blue clapped his hands.

"Three apples long!" Victor said.

Grace laughed, then said, "Stay safe, you guys. And smurf back soon."

They all came together for one large Smurf hug.

"Thank you, once again, Master Winslow," Papa said. Then to Grace, "Miss Doolittle." To the others, "Little Blue—and the Vicster." Papa handed out the crystals. "Let's go home, Smurfs."

"I can't wait to see the rest of my family," Smurfette said. She raised the crystal to her mouth.

"Help!" Vanity interrupted the return trip.

Everyone turned around. Blue had Vanity Smurf stuffed into his mouth. Only his wiggling legs stuck out.

"Blue! No!" Grace shouted.

Patrick pulled out Vanity. He was all wet and slobbery.

Vanity shook off the spit and said, "Okay, here's the

deal. One Smurfberry to everyone to not tell this story."

"Welcome to my world." Grouchy groaned.

Everyone laughed.

"Hey! It's not that funny!" Grouchy was back to his old self.

Chapter 17

The Smurfs were gathered in the center of the village.

POP, POP, POP, POP!

Papa, Clumsy, Grouchy, and Smurfette headed down the hill into town.

"Just as I calculated, Papa's chances of rescuing Smurfette: one hundred percent!" Brainy said proudly.

The other Smurfs rolled their eyes at him.

"And some new Smurfs for our family," Smurfette announced. "Everyone, this is Vexy." She gave Vexy a small push forward.

Everyone froze.

Hefty was in love. "Holy smurfoli! Do they all look like her?"

POP!

Hackus came running into town. "BWAMOOO-AGAGAMOOGA!"

All the Smurfs jumped out of his way.

"Sorry, guys. Can't have everything." Vexy looked around the village and said to Smurfette, "Wow. All these boys."

Smurfette winked. "And just two girls."

"What do you mean?" Vexy asked. "Hackus is a girl."

"Hackus is girl?" Hackus was surprised to hear that. In a flash, Hackus began to chase after Hefty, trying to hug him.

Vexy shouted, "Wait, Hackus! I was kidding!"

Hackus didn't stop. "Hackus don't care. Hackus love family!"

Narrator Smurf stepped up to tell the end of the story. "And so, finally relevant again, our heroic narrator steps back into his leading role to point out that when last we met, the entire village was busying itself with preparations for—"

Smurfette cut in. "Hey, what's with all the decorations?"

"Do you mind? I'm trying to bookend this," Narrator said. "I believe there's a celebration to be had. And so, as the music once again so rudely drowns out the narration—"

The Smurf band began to play, drowning out Narrator again as all the Smurfs cheered, "HAPPY BIRTHDAY, SMURFETTE!"

The Smurfs were going crazy, dancing, singing along. Smurfette jumped up onto the stage, singing her heart out.

Hackus was doing his own jazzy thing. "Scattata-packata-pickita-katata."

Gutsy grabbed a pole and whacked the Gargamel piñata.

Far, far away, Gargamel screamed.

The wizard fell back to Earth from the stratosphere. For a second it looked as though he would land in the reflecting pool at the Trocadéro. But he still had a bit of magic left. Gargamel pointed his wand to slow his fall. The beam of energy hit the water and formed a portal.

With an evil chuckle, Gargamel slammed into the portal . . . and disappeared.

"MEOW!"

Azrael was alone. He meowed again, saying in cat talk, "So long, sucker. The spell is broken! Finally, I'm free of you!" Azrael looked down at the portal. "Are you dead?"

Silence.

He grinned a cat-grin and prepared to take a nap.

Suddenly, a giant blue energy claw reached out of the vortex and grabbed Azrael by the tail.

"Rrrrrrr!"

In a blink, Azrael had gone through the portal with Gargamel to . . . somewhere.